# Praise for Avery Flynn's Books:

"Sexy and sassy... Avery Flynn brings it all."—*Carly Phillips, NY Times Bestselling Author*

"This book is so good you won't want to put it down."—*Harlequin Junkie, Enemies on Tap*

"Flynn intertwines fashionistas and fighters in book two of this heavily talked-about series and she'll leave readers breathless by the time they reach the heart-pounding finish."—*4.5 starts Top Pick, RT Book Reviews, This Year's Black*

Flynn knows her sass and sex ... sheer naughty fun!"—*Into the Fire author Amanda Usen, Betting the Billionaire*

"I loved this story."—*Darynda Jones, NY Times Bestselling Author, Jax and the Beanstalk Zombies*

"...Thrilling, funny  passionate and even contains a few tips to keep the fashion police away from your doorstep."—*RT Book Reviews, High-Heeled Wonder*

# Dangerous Tease

(Laytons Book 3)

By
Avery Flynn

Visit Avery's website at www.averyflynn.com.

Edited by KC
Formatting by Anessa Books

ISBN: 978-0-9908335-5-0 (D) 978-0-9908335-8-1 (P)
Manufactured in the United States of America

First Edition: 2012 (Passion Creek)
Revision: May 2015 (Dangerous Tease)

# Dedication

Finally, it's Sam's turn to find love! I can't tell you how much I've been looking forward to telling his story, but I couldn't have done it without the help of a ton of people. Not that they weigh a ton - well maybe if they all stood together on a scale while holding bricks, but I'm wondering off the path here.

Anyway... I want to thank all of the people who helped make Passion Creek a reality: the fabulous team at Evernight Publishing, Kim and Kerri, whoever thought to turn coffee beans into liquid gold and everyone—yes, everyone—who read the first two books in the Layton Family series, Temptation Creek and Seduction Creek. Y'all rock. Seriously, if there was an Olympics of awesome, you'd all be there.

XOXO,

Avery

# Author Note

Dangerous Tease was first published in 2012 as Passion Creek, but has since been revised.

# Chapter One

$\mathcal{J}$immy "Snips" Esposito smacked his lips together and sucked air through his teeth, his lewd gaze locked on Josie Winarsky's boobs. Still, she managed to bite back a smartass comment. Barely. The guy was a total slimeball, but not one to be messed with—the idea of tangling with a loan shark with mob ties did not make her feel tingly inside. It made her want to puke.

The first time Snips had made the weasel-like sound while hypnotized by her breasts, they'd been sitting in ninth grade English at North Las Vegas High. Snips was still a perv twenty years later, albeit one with more money, bigger muscles and a longer rap sheet.

Of course, her Paris Casino cocktail waitress uniform gave him plenty of tit to ogle, which usually meant big tips—especially in the high-stakes poker rooms. However, after she clocked out for the last time tonight, she planned on burning the damn thing in the parking lot. No more half-in-the-bag, high-stakes poker players' grubby fingers "accidentally" squeezing her ass. No more running from waitressing gig to waitressing gig and eating cheap noodle dinners to save pennies. No more Las Vegas.

In T-minus forty-eight hours, she would be on the road in her duct-taped Honda Civic. Hell or high water wouldn't stop her from getting to the Rose O'Neill Dry Creek Artist Colony and spending the next six months painting.

Only painting.

She'd let those bastards in L.A. rip her dream out of her paint-caked fingers before, but she was stronger now. More determined. Smarter. She'd be damned if she ever let that happen again. Even Snips' hungry little black eyes couldn't fuck up her night.

"Here's your scotch on the rocks." She lowered the glass to the poker table, careful not to let the amber liquid slosh over the rim onto the green felt.

Eyes locked on her fluffed-up chest, he didn't acknowledge the drink.

Josie stood at least four inches taller than Snips in bare feet; add in the heels and she towered over the slimy loan shark. From her vantage point, Josie counted the twelve greasy black hairs slicked over his prematurely bald dome. *And they say God doesn't have a sense of humor.*

"The dealer's about to get started again, but we need to talk later."

"I've told you a million times, Snips, I'm not interested."

"When you hear just how much Cyril owes me, you'll change your tune." Confidence oozed from his blindingly white, toothy grin.

Her baby brother would never borrow money from Snips. "What in the hell are you talking about?"

Snips just smirked. Finally, his eyes met hers. "We'll need to work something out." His gaze dropped again.

"How much?"

Her baby brother by all of twelve minutes had promised the craps games were in his past. Why in the hell would Cy need money from a shark on the lowest rung of the Callandriello family's crime ladder? Was he gambling again in an effort to cover Mom's out-of-whack medical bills? She didn't have the answers. Instead she had an ominous gurgling in the pit of her stomach and Snips' little snake eyes ogling what he could never touch.

Josie wobbled on her four-inch Lucite heels, but forced her voice to strengthen. "I asked how much?"

"Don't worry about it." He winked at her. "I'm sure we can work something out."

She swallowed her disgust. Pointing out the obvious—that Snips wasn't touching, ever—wouldn't help her brother. But she hadn't survived ten years of being a Vegas cocktail waitress by letting creepy little fucks walk all over her.

Leveling an icy glare at Snips, she put on her best bitch-please face, ready to blast him a new one. But Saul Rosenberg shuffled over, lost in a suit jacket that must have fit him in his prime, but now it swam on the man's seventy-year-old frame. Josie ate her words, not wanting to upset her favorite septuagenarian.

Once, after a big tip night, she'd teasingly offered to buy him a new sports coat. His gaze softened and he'd declined, saying his wife had bought it for him on their fortieth anniversary and since Marlene couldn't be here with him, he'd keep the jacket. Josie hadn't been able to stop herself from sighing and giving his frail shoulders a squeeze.

"Josephine, dear." Saul stopped by her elbow, holding a small square package that looked like it had been wrapped by a drunken elephant. "I need a word."

Snips shot her a hard look before turning away.

Josie scanned the room, worried her boss, Clive, would spot her being less than diligent about filling the players' drink orders, but the only person watching her was a long and lean drink of water who, unlike Saul, wasn't a regular at the Paris Casino's high-roller tables. Her gaze locked with his tawny, hazel eyes and her breath caught.

Something woke up within her, setting her pulse racing. The stranger's reddish-brown hair reminded her of her favorite burnt sienna crayon from childhood and her imagination went wild, wondering how this man in his crisp shirt and pressed jeans got the two-inch scar that wriggled across his cheekbone. His fingers wrapped around the old fashioned glass. Josie had no idea how his drink stayed so cold because she was burning up just looking at him.

His aesthetic was all alpha man—broad shoulders, muscular arms and lean, strong fingers. Her gaze traveled back up to his face and her skin sizzled as his hazel eyes stayed focused on her. He didn't smile and, judging by the tense line of his jaw, rarely did. Too bad; if his smile matched the rest of him, it would be a sight to behold. She wished he'd stand up so she could see if his ass was as squeeze-worthy as her mind painted.

On canvas, he would fill the space, muscles coiled, battle-ready. A painting of him bloomed in her mind: a Spartan warrior, fierce and deadly, gearing up for war. A shiver started at the base of her spine and ended when her shoulders twitched, jiggling her barely contained boobs.

She never slept with her customers, too many were regulars and she didn't believe in making relationship ties. But this guy wasn't a regular and for him, she might just break her own golden rule. After all, it was her last night on the job. She stepped in his direction.

"Josephine, did you hear what I said?"

Her cheeks flushed and she turned. "I'm sorry, Mr. Rosenberg. It's my last night and I'm a little out of sorts."

"Understandable." He patted her hand with his own liver-spotted one. "I got you a gift."

"Oh, you shouldn't—"

"Shhh, playing poker and discussing art are my only loves now that Marlene has passed on. I couldn't let you go without thanking you for listening to me prattle on about both."

Those stories had always circled back around to his beloved Marlene. The widower had spun tales of everyday romance, like bringing home flowers on Thursdays, and continuing to do so out of habit even after his wife died. It was the stuff of books and movies, not real life—at least not as she knew it. Between two waitressing jobs and spending every nonworking waking moment with a paintbrush in her hand, a relationship was so far on the back burner, it wasn't even in the kitchen.

He held out the package. "Go on, unwrap it."

Josie bit the inside of her cheek and tore the thin wrapping paper to reveal a small book. The musty scent of old paper and worn leather wafted up. She slid her thumb across the battered corner of the crackled cover.

"It's Dry Creek, Nebraska. That's where you're going, yes?"

"Right. They've got a great artist colony. I'm going to spend six months painting."

"I thought so. Turn to the first page."

She eased open the cover, afraid the obviously old book would tear. *Diary of Rebecca Morrell, Dry Creek Nebraska, 1865.* Josie traced her fingers across the bold but faded script.

"I won it a few years ago in a poker match. The young man said it had been in his family for generations. It seems young Rebecca was crossing the country on the Oregon Trail with her dowry to meet her fiancé out West. She made it as far as Nebraska when she discovered he'd died. Heartbroken, she stayed in Dry Creek, where she eventually married a rancher."

"How sad." Like a real sap, her heart winced at the tale.

"Yes, but according to the young man and what's in here..." He tapped the diary with one arthritic finger. "She buried her dowry outside of Dry Creek. Many have looked for Rebecca's Bounty, as they call it, but none have found it."

"I'm not surprised."

"But they didn't have the map. You do."

Her breath hitched. A real treasure meant money, maybe enough to pay off her mother's medical bills, Snips and a longer stay in Dry Creek. "Map?"

"Oh yes, I took the diary to be appraised and the examiner found the map secreted in a false flap on the back cover. It took me a while to realize it's a map. I thought it was just some lovely drawings— Rebecca, it seems, was an artist herself—but then one day it hit me. She'd drawn a treasure map hidden inside her landscape drawings. Quite a clever girl, that Rebecca. My Marlene would have liked her."

"Mr. Rosenberg, this gift is truly lovely, thank you, but it must be valuable. I can't accept this." She held out the book, but he waved off her offer.

"It is worth money but I'm too old to go on any more adventures; however, you're certainly not. Take it with you to Dry Creek. Who knows, maybe you'll be the one to find Rebecca's Bounty. If nothing else, think of it as the diary of a fellow artist and a reminder of an old man who enjoyed your company."

She swallowed the sentiment blocking her throat. "Thank you."

After a quick hug, he shuffled back to his poker table and she hid the diary in a safe spot behind the bar.

Mr. Tall Drink of Water sat a few chairs away from Saul, deep in conversation with the man on his left. The other guy looked a few years younger, relaxed and mellow, unlike the man who put an extra bit of sway in her hips as she strutted toward the players. He had an air of alertness about him and an intensity that couldn't be missed. Still, the resemblance between the two men—from their broad shoulders to their matching hazel eyes—left little doubt they were related. Both were handsome, but there was something about the older one that sent a tingle sprinting across her exposed skin as surely as if he'd touched her. She couldn't wait to get close enough for better inspection.

"Hey ya," a burly player called out from Saul's table. "Bring me a Jack and Coke."

Yanked back into reality, Josie made a beeline toward the bar and away from the six-feet-plus of yumminess getting ready for another round of Texas Hold 'Em.

Hours later, her size-ten feet aching, she leaned against the bar and counted down the minutes of her final shift in the world's most uncomfortable shoes. She'd probably get cancer from the hazardous toxins released if she burned them with her uniform. Maybe she'd just run them over a couple thousand times with her battered Honda instead. Of course, with her luck, the Lucite heels would puncture the worn tread on the tires.

The itch of a thousand ants marching up her arms tipped her off that she hadn't gone unnoticed in the empty bar corner farthest from the poker tables. Only one person gave her the heebie-jeebies quite like this. She turned. Bingo.

Snips stood just shy of her personal bubble.

"Okay, how much does Cy owe?"

"Forty K."

Her blood pressure exploded. "Why in the hell would he need forty thousand dollars?" *Please God, don't say he's found a craps game that would take him.*

Snips shrugged. "Don't know. Don't care. I just want my money, but your brother dropped off the radar. That does not inspire my confidence. If he doesn't show up soon, I'm going to have to track him down as a message to the rest of my clients." It went without saying that Snips' threats involved baseball bats and brass knuckles. "So where is he?"

Her stomach clenched. Something was off. Way off. After Mom got really sick, Cy had cleaned up his act and joined the military. He'd left the Corps a few months ago, but was being all mysterious about how he was supporting himself. Warning sirens blared in her head.

"I haven't heard from him in a few days. I don't know where he is."

"Well, I hope you have an extra forty thousand stuffed between those big tits of yours." He raised up on his toes and leered at her.

"I bet you do." She crossed her arms to block his view.

He guffawed, an ugly, mean sound. "You'd better find my money or your brother. I'd hate to have to go introduce myself to your parents. Haven't seen your mom since high school. She still in the wheelchair? I really should stop by and see how her kidney dialysis is going."

Panic buzzed inside Josie's head like a kamikaze bee on a suicide mission. Her mom would give her last penny to help Cy. Shit, she'd already done it about a million times, that was why Josie had come home from L.A. Well, one of the reasons. But Mom couldn't afford to do it now, not with a foot-high stack of medical bills and a mile-wide stubborn streak pushing her to refuse any financial help from Josie.

No, she'd have to take care of this before her parents even heard about it.

"Look, I don't have it all, but I'll get it. I just need some time. Come by the diner during the lunch shift tomorrow and I'll give you five grand." Just saying the words was like watching her dreams curl up and die.

Snips' eyes lit up, no doubt at the prospect of getting his grubby hands on her hard-earned cash.

That money was her entire life savings after she'd paid for her stay at the Rose O'Neill Dry Creek

Artist Colony, but if Cy was desperate enough to borrow money from Snips, he really needed it. The fact that he'd dropped out of sight meant something had gone very wrong and he was in real trouble. Damn, why hadn't she followed up on his last cryptic text? He'd promised to never leave her to clean up his messes again—unless something awful had happened.

"I need it all." Snips snuck across the invisible line separating her space from his. "Of course, you're such a hot piece of ass that I could be persuaded to give you a few extra weeks, if you asked in the right way."

The ants double-timed across her skin and she took an involuntary half-step back. "Come on, we've known each other since middle school. I've told you a million times, no way, no how."

Anger flashed in his beady eyes. "Yeah and in all that time, Miss Tight Ass, you've never given me a second glance or the respect I deserve. I was never good enough for you. But guess who needs me now?" He raised himself on his tiptoes and jutted his face into hers. "Who's hot shit now, bitch?"

His hand shot out so fast it must have broken some kind of land-speed record and clamped onto her left breast.

Shock stopped the moment in time. Her brain emptied until it was a vast white space with only one thought: What. The. Fuck?

He kneaded her tit like a baker with a loaf of unformed dough.

Rage and disgust rattled and climbed up to her throat, her cheeks flamed. She gritted her teeth and shoved his hand away, her knee slamming into his steroid-shrunken balls. He bent over with an *oomph*! She grabbed the metal serving tray in both hands and swung it with everything her five-foot-eleven-inch body could give. The tray made a heavy boing sound on the side of his head.

He went down. Hard.

Lungs heaving, she tried to bring her breathing and heart rate back to normal while her brother's loan shark—the man who held Cy's kneecaps in his hands—wriggled on the ground in agony.

The other poker players, waitresses and even the new bartender let out a collective gasp. Pandemonium broke out as the crowd converged around them. Mr. Tall Drink of Water hung back, but he tipped an invisible hat at her. Shouted questions bounced off the walls.

"What the hell happened, Josie?" Her boss, Clive, picked that moment to appear.

"He grabbed my boob."

"Aw, hell." He swiped his fingers through his hair and aged about ten years in a breath. Snips dropped a ton of cash at the casino on a regular basis. "Go change and then let's talk in my office."

Clive went to work dispersing the gawkers.

*Fuckity fuck fuck.* And this was why Cy rolled his eyes at her whenever she called him out about his temper.

Snips staggered up, holding his junk with both hands. An apricot-sized goose egg deformed his round head.

"You fuckin' cunt." Spittle sprayed from his angry mouth. Hatred and pain twisted his face. "Forty thousand dollars. I want it all. Tomorrow."

He limped to the door and out to the Paris Casino's general gambling floor.

Well, she'd taken the bad and made it about twenty times worse. *Way to go, Josie.* She had less than twenty-four hours to find Cy, or cash out her life savings and find an additional thirty-five thousand dollars. Bile rose in her throat. The tray slid from her clammy grasp.

She could sell her car. Work extra shifts in the poker room and at the diner. Forget about Dry Creek. Maybe she could get a refund.

Her shoulders slumped. Exhaling a deep breath, she headed for the employee locker room. There was no time for feeling sorry for herself. As her dad, a lifelong plumber, said, life doesn't always give you copper pipes, sometimes it just gives you shit.

Swiping the diary from its hiding spot, she gave herself a mental shake then marched out of the poker room.

Sinking down onto a metal folding chair in the employee locker room, she tried to steady her shaking hands enough to unbuckle her shoes. It took three tries, but she finally got them undone and tossed them into her duffel, then wriggled out of her miniscule uniform. So much for the bonfire she'd been planning. Josie sniffled back a tear. She couldn't stop her bottom lip from quivering, but dammit, she would not actually cry. It wouldn't change anything.

Pulling on a pair of dark denim jeans and tugging a soft cotton T-shirt over her head, she contemplated her next task: persuading Clive to give her some more shifts in the poker room. It would take a whole lot of fast talk to get him to agree. Lately, he'd been overwhelmed with requests for overtime from everyone and Josie had three things working against her. She stuffed the diary in her backpack and swung it over one shoulder, grabbed her duffel bag in her other hand and cataloged the negative marks.

One, she'd already quit.

Two, unlike most of the waitresses, her twenties were a fast-fading memory.

And three, she'd just whacked a high roller and kicked him in the nuts.

Desperation tightened around her neck with each step on the short walk from the locker room to Clive's office. She had better odds at the slot machine than she did sweet-talking her boss into giving her more hours. Good luck with that.

He answered her knock before Josie's knuckles even broke contact with the door. A red blotch colored his Adam's apple. Clive only got the hives when he'd been on the business end of a reaming.

"What a way to end your last shift." He scurried around his desk and flopped into his chair.

"About that—"

He held up his hand. "You already handed in your notice. This was your last day."

Even though she'd expected it, her stomach sank. "Something came up. I changed my mind, can't you—"

"Jimmy 'Snips' Esposito went to the top. Shit, he dialed the CEO before he even hit the front door. They assured him tonight was your last night."

"But he grabbed me!"

"He disputes that and no one witnessed the incident."

"The security cameras—"

"Won't have seen anything. They *never* see anything when it comes to him." He shrugged his shoulders. "I'm sorry, Josie, but it is what it is."

Her body ached, every organ and limb hurt. A bone-deep sense of exhaustion swamped her. She didn't even have the energy to be pissed off. Everything had tumbled down on top of her like a house of cards. Just like L.A. The memory of that betrayal struggled to emerge from a lockbox in the back of her mind but she had enough practice ignoring the pain to force it back. She'd find a way out of this mess. She'd done it before. She'd do it again.

Josie spun on her heel and walked out the door, leaving her tacky-ass uniform in the duffle bag on the floor in front of Clive's desk.

# Chapter Two

$\mathcal{T}$wenty minutes later, Josie sank back onto a barstool near the casino's off-track betting room, desperate for a little girl talk with her best friend, Mike, who was tending bar. He'd handed her the usual vodka gimlet and hurried off to tend the customers at the other end of the bar. She twisted away from the raucous trio of blondes at the other end of the room whose last sober moment must have been hours ago—if not days.

Lucky them, everything was perfect in their lives. Damn, she sure sounded like a bitter little muffin with a forty thousand dollar debt tied around her neck. *Must be the gimlets.* She snorted at her own bad joke.

The first crisp, ice-cold vodka with a hint of lime in the  had gone down way too easy. Josie really didn't care as she accepted the second that Mike slid her way. She'd already left Cy four voicemails. Her texts had gone unanswered. No one in the family had heard from him in a week. Not since Cy had e-mailed that he'd hooked up with a construction crew for a two-week job in Reno. Her twin vibe would be going mad if something had happened to him, like it had when he was shot in Iraq. She'd known hours before the call came. But this time, baby bro just didn't want to talk.

"Hell, if I owed pond scum forty thousand, I'd probably be ignoring my phone too," she mumbled into her drink.

Still, a nugget of worry sat like a brick in her stomach. Why would Cy need to borrow money, let alone that much?

Stymied in her search for the answers, she took refuge in another gulp of vodka. After everything that had happened in the past few hours, some adult beverages and a bitch session with Mike were in order. Hashing it out with her best friend always seemed to set things clear in her head.

She'd accomplished step one, having a pair of vodka gimlets. Step two had been a bust because of the bachelorette party. The small casino bar was normally deserted at this time since most games had finished hours ago, but tonight Mike had slid the second gimlet her way then gone back to making a trio of pink martinis. He set the drinks on the bar in front of the flirty blondes and made his way toward Josie on the opposite end.

"Sorry, doll, you know what bachelorette parties are like—high maintenance but with an equally big tip. All I have to do is pour the drinks and bat my eyelashes."

"Don't you feel the least bit guilty?"

He shrugged. "For what?"

"Flirting with horny drunk girls when you're gay?"

Mike arched a perfectly shaped eyebrow and blew her a kiss with lips that had never touched female flesh, except to kiss his mother on the cheek at Thanksgiving. "Honey, when I flirt, it is a form of high art. They could care less who I go home with."

Judging by the lust reflected in the bride-to-be's glassy eyes, she just might.

"Oh, Mikey, I need some help." The woman tilted her head and pouted.

"Well, I do believe I have just what you need." He winked at Josie then sauntered down to the other end of the bar to earn an extra zero on his tip.

Eh, who could blame him? It wasn't as if Josie didn't do the same thing with the poker players. Scratch that. She used to do the same thing. Now she was an underemployed waitress with only one job, a perv loan shark circling her for forty K and a brother in the wind.

Josie twirled the skinny brown straw in her second gimlet and the ice cubes clinked against the glass. She planned on savoring this one, as it would likely be her last frivolous purchase for the foreseeable future. Tomorrow, she'd track down Cy, pick up as many extra shifts at the diner as she could and put a listing for her car on Craigslist. After that...well...she didn't have the energy to think about it but that's what family did, they saved each other when the situation called for it. She'd find a way.

The stool next to her slid back.

Except for her, Mike and the bachelorette party, the entire bar held nothing but empty chairs. Yet someone had to pick the barstool right next to her? She really was not in the mood to deal with a chatty tourist right now.

Determined to wallow alone in her own misery for at least one more gimlet, she kept her head down and her body turned slightly away.

Then, out of the corner of her eye, she watched Mr. Tall Drink of Water from the poker room sit down.

Her heart started doing jumping jacks and, all of a sudden, hanging out alone feeling sorry for herself lost much of its appeal. Josie's pulse jackhammered in her throat and she squirmed on her barstool. Keeping her face angled down, she used her peripheral vision to scope him out. Tall. Strong without being a musclebound goon. Light reddish-brown hair worn long enough to show the beginnings of a slight wave. He smiled her way and her cheeks blazed at being caught.

"You okay after what happened?"

His voice slid across her skin like warm, poisonous honey, dangerous but oh so sweet.

And, poof, gone was her vodka-induced acceptance of her current no-win situation. Anxiety and anger one-two punched her in the solar plexus as hard as she'd whacked Snips with the serving tray.

"Perfectly fine. Getting felt up by the gamblers is just one of the many perks of being a drink bunny."

"Sounds like a shitty job."

She snorted and picked up her glass, its condensation cooling her palm. Sure, it was a craptastic job, but the tips were huge and she needed to make bank fast.

"*Was* a shitty job. And since jobs are just so plentiful around here, I won't have any problem finding another," Josie said, sarcasm thick in her tone. She gulped back a swallow, the clear liquid burning down her throat. As drawn to this stranger as she was, another in a short string of one-night stands wasn't a good idea tonight. Her emotions lay too close to the surface, bubbling and threatening to overflow.

"Good for you for quitting."

"Oh, I didn't quit. They fired me."

"Fired you?" His voice dropped an octave, becoming deadly serious.

"Correction. They declined to accept my change of heart about my resignation. Tonight was supposed to be my last night, but then my world went to hell and I realized I had to keep my two awful waitressing jobs, beg for overtime and give up my dream, all to fix Cy's mess. Brothers, they really can make your life hell sometimes." Josie sucked in a shaky breath, realizing too late she was about two seconds from crying in front of a total stranger about the shit pit her life had become.

Forget talking to Mike later, she needed to beat feet before she turned into a blubbering mess in public. She hopped off the stool, swiped her backpack off the floor and tried her best to level her voice. "Look, I'm sorry. I shouldn't have dumped all over you, it's just been...well, you know what it's been."

Trying to salvage her shredded pride, Josie took two steps toward the door before a hand on her shoulder stopped her. His heat seeped into her, sparking a trail of fire from his thumb on her shoulder blade to the juncture of her thighs. Josie turned and faced him.

"I'm Sam Layton. Why don't you let me buy you a drink?"

Mesmerized by the golden hazel of his heavily hooded eyes, she could only nod her assent. Dangerous territory ahead, her sense of self-preservation counseled, but she ignored the warning.

Sam couldn't let her walk out now even if Rebecca's Bounty had been laid out in his hotel room. The draw was immediate and undeniable, but that didn't mean it was logical or close to typical behavior for him.

His type ran quiet; academic women with hair pulled tight and shirts buttoned to the throat. Women whose most passionate outbursts came during faculty meetings at Cather College about publishing requirements for tenure. Neither he nor his dates stuck out in the crowd like this platinum Amazon.

The mixed scent of amber and orange wafted around her, teasing his senses. Without thinking about why, he scooted his barstool closer to hers when she sat back down.

"Josie Winarsky." Her gray eyes stared into him. His face must have reflected his inner confusion because her Ferrari-red lips curled into a smile. "My name, it's Josie."

"Like the song?"

She shook her head, sending the fat curls that fell to her chin waving. "Oh, I hate that song."

"Too late now, it's stuck in my head. Josie's on a vacation far away..." Who was this person singing in a bar? Even his own mother wouldn't recognize him.

Not that he didn't want to flirt, because Josie was gorgeous. She must've been almost six feet tall with legs that went on and on like an epic poem. She'd changed out of her cocktail outfit, but he couldn't stop picturing the intricate, tattooed curving vines and flowers that twisted into the shape of an infinity sign spanning from one bare shoulder to the next. He'd been so busy watching those vines while he played poker, he'd folded on a royal flush.

Only a moron did that, which, apparently, included him tonight.

The plain white T-shirt she wore now covered that tattoo, along with almost all of a tiny pink princess slaying a kelly-green dragon on her right biceps. Only the dragon's curled tail extended below her sleeve.

"What'll you have?" The bartender in a tight black shirt winked at Josie.

"Another gimlet, thanks, Mike."

"You got it, kitten. How 'bout you?"

"Scotch, neat."

Mike wandered off to make their drinks, leaving Josie and Sam in the middle of an awkward silence. His shirt collar felt tight. He undid the top button. After all, he was in Vegas—he might as well live a little.

"What do you do, Sam?"

"I'm a history professor."

"Oh, I love American history. I just read the most fascinating book about Cleveland's assassination."

He'd yet to get to that new release, which was sitting on a stack of books on his nightstand. "Really?"

She narrowed her eyes. "Why? Do you think drink fairies with big tits only read the tabloids and TMZ?"

"That's not what I meant." His cheeks flamed. This was why he never flirted. Foot in mouth seemed to be his specialty outside of the lecture hall.

"Uh-huh." She took her gimlet from Mike, the ice cubes clinking as she sipped. A red copy of her lips stayed on the glass when she put it down. "So are you at UNLV?"

"No, Cather College."

"Where's that?"

"Dry Creek, Nebraska."

Her face darkened and her spine stiffened.

What the hell had he done now?

Desperate not to sink into silence again, he grasped for a conversation topic. The black ink script on the inside of her left wrist caught his eye. "What does it say?"

Her brows squeezed together in a question before she smiled softly and held out her wrist to him.

Sam brushed his thumb across the blue veins visible under her porcelain skin. Electricity jolted against his fingertips, tingling its way up his arm. His lungs tightened and his cock stirred. From his position, the words were upside down. Without letting go of Josie's wrist, he stepped down from his stool and turned so that they faced the same direction, with her directly behind him.

They were so close, her breasts rubbed against his back. "Sam…"

The single syllable brushed against the back of his neck and his body reacted as if she'd caressed his dick instead of only speaking his name. He wouldn't, couldn't, let go of her until he read the tattoo. He had to know what it said.

*Adventure is worthwhile in itself.*

"Amelia Earhart." He lifted her wrist to his mouth, kissing the words as her pulse jumped under his lips. Surrounded by her amber scent, touching her soft skin, tasting her warmth on his lips, the out-of-character action seemed perfectly logical.

Josie slid her arm from his grasp and he reluctantly returned to his stool. But she didn't leave or scoot farther away.

"How did you know?" Her long fingers stroked across her wrist.

"My dissertation was about Earhart's impact on Midwestern women's perspectives of early twentieth century feminism."

She arched her brow. "An unusual topic for a dude."

"You haven't met my family. If you aren't comfortable with strong women, you won't last long." He fell deeper into her orbit at the sound of her alto laugh. "How about you, what's your story?"

"I'm a waitress, remember?"

"Bullshit. That's a job, it's not who you are. Come on, if you can't spill your secrets to a total and complete stranger whom you'll never see again, whom can you tell?"

A lightness loosened her tense shoulders. She leaned in closer. "Sort of an *I'll tell you mine, if you tell me yours*, eh?"

Blood rushed in Sam's ears before heading south. "Exactly."

She laughed and began telling him about growing up in Vegas with her mom, dad and brother. As she talked, she played with the simple gold chain around her neck that dipped down into her creamy cleavage. The sight of her fingers tangling in the delicate necklace entranced him, taunted him with visions of her touching him. He had no clue how long he sat in a desire-induced daze before she caught him.

"Sam, did you hear a word I just said?" She laughed, a low, throaty sound that ratcheted up the lust fogging his brain.

He had no idea where she was in her story when he'd stopped listening. "You caught me."

"And I was just telling you the story about how a nude modeling gig during art school turned into a crazy all-night orgy." Her teasing tone gave away the statement as a whopper.

"I'm really sorry to have missed that. Can you tell it again?"

She tossed back her head and laughed, sending her platinum curls bouncing.

For the next few hours they talked about their families, debated American political history, discussed her painting and laughed at the escalating—and doomed—flirtation between Mike and the trio of bachelorettes. Somehow their barstools moved closer and closer until their legs touched from ankles to hips. While his higher mental functions were focused on talking, the rest of him reveled in the softness of her skin, the way she chewed on the short straw from her gimlet and the top curve of her breasts peeking out from her V-neck T-shirt.

She wet her lips with a swipe of her pink tongue and his cock almost broke through his zipper. Her fingers brushed against his biceps and he had to force himself not to toss her over his shoulder and race up to his room. Wondering if that soft spot where her hip dipped in to meet her waist tasted as sweet as her wrist was about to drive him crazy.

"Am I boring you?"

Caught in fantasy land again, he shook his head.

Her hand dropped to his thigh, searing his skin through the thick denim of his jeans.

"Not at all." He squeezed the words out from between gritted teeth. "Just momentarily distracted."

Her gray eyes sparkled and even though her fingers stayed closer to his knee than his crotch, he swore she knew exactly how uncomfortably distracted he'd become.

"Whatcha thinkin' about?" She leaned in, giving him an excellent view of her bountiful cleavage.

He sputtered out the first thing that came to mind. "Your tattoos."

"Oh yeah?" Her hand traveled north. "Let's go up to your room so I can show them all to you."

# Chapter Three

*J*ust kissing Sam's lips and tasting the smoky peat-flavored scotch lingering there wasn't enough. Josie needed to touch him. Everywhere.

Now.

They'd barely made it through the door of his hotel room before she'd wrestled his shirt tails free of his waistband. She slid her fingers underneath to tangle in the dusting of mahogany hair leading to the button on his jeans. His abs jumped under her touch. Need flared to life between her legs. Their lips locked together, forcing out every thought in her brain. He electrified her body, every cell alive with wanting.

This is what she needed: to escape in the arms of a stranger and forget about the sword hanging over her head. No emotion. No ties. No happily ever after. Just hot, heady fucking.

The hotel room door thunked closed and Sam pulled away, the inches separating their lips seeming like miles. Their chests heaved in unison, her diamond-hard nipples tenting underneath the soft cotton of her T-shirt.

His finger sketched a meandering line down the column of her neck, pausing for a moment at her frantic pulse point before continuing along through the deep valley between her heavy breasts.

The gimlets couldn't take credit for the firestorm of sensation. It was all Sam. His deliberate pace became blissful torture. She pressed his large hand against her overheated skin.

His fingers dipped under her V-neck, resting on the uppermost swell of her tits, but didn't move; their stillness more erotic than if he'd reached farther down to caress her straining nipples.

Sam swung her up in his arms as if she were a tiny, delicate thing. Hardly anyone challenged her dominant, bitch-please attitude, but he marched across the room with her as if he had every right and tossed her onto the bed. The change was freeing. She sank back into the soft, thick comforter, ready and ravenous for him. All of him.

He stood by the side of the king-size bed, watching her with a hungry look that emphasized the tiger-gold of his eyes. His long, strong lines tempted her to grab a pencil and make a quick sketch of a man starving for something more. Something hard and rough. But the throbbing between her legs overruled her artistic instinct. Later, she'd paint him half-dressed and hard. Everywhere.

He made quick work of the buttons on his conservative pale-blue shirt, revealing a sprinkling of brown hair tinged with dawn's orange. Her gaze traveled down to his cock pushing against its denim prison. Time for a jailbreak.

She rose to her knees and reached for his jeans, her tongue tasting the indent above his hipbone. If her history professors had looked like him in college, she would never have skipped class. Her fingers, clumsy with lust, fumbled with the stiff button while her mouth explored the hard plane of his stomach. Despite spending the past few hours in the Paris Casino's smoky bar, he smelled of warm leather, cinnamon and something she couldn't place at first.

It hit her at the same moment she wriggled his button through the hole—a new book, cracked open for the first time.

Holding her breath, she lowered his zipper at a turtle's pace, wanting to draw out the anticipation as he'd done for her, to take him to the same nearly delirious plane. The end result did not disappoint. Thick, hard and heavy, his dick was a woman's fantasy cock. She wrapped her fingers around his girth and lowered her head to lick the salty pre-cum from its tip.

Sam's fingers threaded through her hair. "If you do any more of that, I won't be able to control myself."

She stroked him, enjoying its iron smoothness. "Control is highly overrated."

He groaned and slid her up his hard body, until they were face-to-face. There was nothing sweet or soft about his kiss. Hard and demanding, it shot flames of need through her body. Her clit ached to be touched. She couldn't wait any longer.

Josie broke the kiss long enough to pull her T-shirt over her head and drop it to the floor, then sought his lips again. The air crackled around them with anticipation and something more—a yearning she hadn't experienced before.

They tumbled onto the bed. He swept one arm outward, shoving the overabundance of pillows to the floor. There were no words. Hands moved everywhere. Touching. Stroking. Squeezing. Tension in her stomach pulled tighter. Clothes disappeared, replaced by a condom that for all Josie knew had appeared out of thin air.

Her nipples hardened under his tongue. She writhed on the bed. His fingers traced lines down her sides, stopping at her hips and leaving a trail of fire on her damp skin. She wrapped her legs around his waist, twining her ankles at the small of his back, her heels pressing him forward.

"Fuck me, Sam, I can't wait."

He growled in answer, a mix of triumph and relief that put her on the edge of coming undone. His buttoned-up exterior hid something wild, and she loved being the one to set it free. That they could both find a kind of escape tangled in the crisp white sheets of a hotel bed made the night even better.

Sam pressed his face into the curve where her shoulder met her neck. His teeth nipped at the tender skin and he slid into her wet pussy in one deep thrust. Pleasure ricocheted through her body. Her back arched like a bow. Their fingers intertwined, staying bound together even as their bodies separated and joined at an ever-quickening pace.

With a quick twist, she flipped him onto his back and rode him until her thighs burned. Sweat slicked, she bent backwards and grabbed her ankles, the angle allowing him to slide deeper, as if he'd always belonged embedded inside her.

Her climax started like an electric ball of energy in her lower back, enlarging in waves until her entire body buzzed. Sam groaned as he withdrew and entered, going deeper than before. The charged sphere snapped, her orgasm exploding like a lightning bolt with his body stiffening a moment later.

They collapsed next to each other, his arm draped across the curve of her waist. Eyes closed in a sublime state of relaxation, Josie promised herself she'd sneak off as soon as Sam's breath steadied with sleep. She'd just close her eyes for a minute.

Sam shifted beside her, bringing the fluffy comforter down over the two of them and securing her closer against his side. A weak SOS signaled from deep within, prodding her to stick to standard operating procedure, but she squeezed her eyes shut against it. The bed was too comfortable, the moment too easy and the man too perfect of a fit.

However, the more she ignored that inner voice, the louder it became, until it blared like a foghorn. Prodded by the self-preservation habits made over the past decade, Josie unwrapped herself from their warm cocoon and sat up.

"Don't go." His fingers stretched across her taut thigh.

"I have to."

Josie glanced over her shoulder at Sam, who had turned on his side to watch her. The fast flutter in her chest confirmed that somewhere between the bar and the bed, this had moved beyond the usual fuck-'em-and-leave-'em routine into something more interesting.

"Do you want to go?"

"No." The word escaped before she could come up with one of her usual cover stories about an early work shift or her nonexistent dog that had to be walked because, for once, no was the truth.

"Then stay."

His plea hung in the air until she relaxed back onto the bed.

Sam traced the tattooed vines winding across Josie's shoulders and followed as they dipped lower, shadowing her spine and ending in another infinity symbol on the small of her back, right above the matching dimples at the top of her round ass.

She shivered under his fingers. "That tickles."

"It's so...pretty." So much for being able to use his Scrabble-worthy vocabulary.

He buried his nose in her soft hair, her curls like silk against his cheeks, and inhaled her amber scent. His cock stirred in response. Ducking his head lower, he kissed the infinity sign's center.

"My friend is a tattoo artist so I get a discount."

"Did he design this?" Sam kissed the spot on her shoulder blade where the vines passed closest to her freckled shoulders.

She sighed and snuggled her ass closer to his stiffening cock. "Nah. I draw them up and he traces them onto my skin before inking me."

"Even the princess and the dragon?"

"Yeah. I got that right before my first show." She laughed, a dry sound with more than a touch of disappointment "I thought I'd finally slain the dragon."

He pulled her closer to him as they spooned and kissed her shoulder. "What happened?"

"A so-called friend stole my art and the original sketches then passed it off as her own at a gallery in L.A." Her husky voice went silent.

"Did you say anything?"

"Yeah, not that it did any good. Her rich parents had so many deep connections in that world that no one believed me." Her shoulders slumped. "You don't want to hear this. We're both old enough to know that life doesn't work out like you think it will when you're young, now does it?"

She sighed and Sam wished he could erase the disillusionment in her voice. "It's not over for you yet."

"Well, Dry Creek is long gone, that's for sure."

His pulse hiccupped. "Dry Creek, Nebraska?" Blasting out of his comfort zone with someone like Josie in Vegas was one thing. It was quite another to do that back home in a small town that thrived on gossip—especially gossip concerning the Laytons. Everyone and his mother would be taking notes.

"Yeah, there's an artist colony there. I was going to paint until my fingers fell off, but it doesn't look like I'll be able to go. I'm just hoping they'll refund the money I've already paid."

He'd no more than released a relieved breath than guilt twisted him. "That's...that's too bad," he stuttered.

Josie rolled over in his arms, her gray eyes soft. "It would have been nice to go knowing that there was somebody there I knew." She smirked at him and traced her finger down the scar on his cheek he'd gotten that summer on McPherson's Bluff. "We could have even gone treasure hunting together."

His entire body tensed. "What are you talking about?" The blood iced in his veins.

He should have known. Treasure hunters had been after the Layton family treasure, Rebecca's Bounty, for decades. They wouldn't think twice about using any means necessary to gather information. Even sleeping with the one family member who'd spent decades looking for it. God knows more than a few had tried to get close to him in hopes of getting a look at Rebecca's diary or other family relics.

"Were you waiting for me, Josie? How long have you been watching me?"

Josie sat up, the sheet falling to her narrow waist. "What in the hell are you talking about?"

Despite the temper building, he couldn't stop his gaze from straying to her pendulous breasts.

"The treasure." Gold, jewels and who knew what else buried somewhere outside of Dry Creek. He'd been raised on the legend. Lost his belief in happy endings while searching for it the summer he turned twelve. Michael's last August. Regret and anger tag-teamed his chest, squeezing his lungs tight until he could barely breathe.

"You are completely off your nut." She threw the covers off long legs that had wrapped so tightly around him. "God, why do I always attract the weirdoes?"

He refused to let her off that easy. "Don't try to distract and discredit. Who hired you?" Uncle Harlan was his first suspect, but there were others.

"That's it. Have a nice life." She jumped off the bed and made a beeline for her clothes.

How could he have been so wrong about her? Usually his instincts were pretty good, but something about Josie had fucked-up his compass as badly as if it had been placed on a slab of iron.

Now dressed, Josie stomped over to the chair and grabbed her backpack. The zipper must have been open because its contents spilled out onto the chair and scattered on floor. Her shoulders shook as if she was trying not to cry.

Doubt niggled at Sam. A born cynic, he never bought the company line and always expected the worst. What if he hadn't been wrong about Josie? What if she didn't know anything about Rebecca's Bounty? He didn't have any proof, just natural-born suspicion. Fuck. He couldn't leave it like this.

"Let me help."

"Stop." Her order cut through the room. "I can do it myself." She gathered up a small book, cards and an extra pair of shoes and shoved them into the bag.

Without another word, she stormed out of the hotel room and out of his life.

He slumped down in a chair, gut aching like he'd gone *mano a mano* against a giant. When had he become such a prick? He couldn't blame a failed treasure hunt for that.

An image of twelve-year-old Michael looking up with death staring out from those familiar hazel eyes flashed in Sam's mind and bile rose in his throat. The memories always came back when he forgot to be vigilant. The more orderly his life, the less Michael haunted him, so Sam had worked hard to create a life of black and white with no colors in between. Being with Josie and her riot of hues had jostled the memories loose.

Sam shifted in the chair and paper crackled underneath him. In a haze, he pulled it out and unfolded the yellowed page.

Charcoal landscape sketches filled the page. A natural rock bridge. Stubby sagebrush trees barely hanging on to a stone ledge with the expansive prairie pouring out into the distance. A rocky formation towering above a flat, barren field with a glimpse of craggy badlands peeking out from behind. A small inscription had been scrawled in the corner.

*There is a beauty to this hard land more valuable than treasure, but for those who insist, I give you this. Rebecca, 1865.*

It took a minute for its meaning to hit him.

"Holy shit."

Rumors had circulated for years about a treasure map but he'd never found it despite searching. While plenty of fakes had turned up, the real one remained elusive. Sam scanned the paper, taking in the quality, the discoloration, the unique script that at first glance matched Rebecca's writings. He wouldn't know for sure until he got back home to compare it with other documents in his collection, but this had all the markings of the fabled treasure map for Rebecca's Bounty.

How the hell did Josie get it? His uncle had lost the diary in a poker match ten years ago.

The contents of his stomach curdled. The small book she'd shoved into her backpack. The whole fucking thing had been a setup.

Josie hadn't been interested in him. No. She wanted a Layton to pump for information for some fool's errand and he'd walked right into the trap—until he'd called her out. People had been searching for his great-great-great-great-grandmother's treasure since before his father had been born.

His gaze caught on the jeans he'd ironed that morning lying in a puddle by the bed and anger blazed through him.

He should have known better.

Josie jammed the elevator down button with her finger, then poked it again and again for good measure.

Paranoid asshole. This was why she stuck with no-strings-attached, one-night stands. She had the personality judgment skills of a gullible puppy.

This wasn't the first time she'd been screwed by her missing bullshit detector. Getting fired, Cy's huge debt and the fresh wound Sam had inflicted revived old hurts, allowing the worst of them to break to the surface.

The long-buried pain sliced through her so sharply and with such strength, she could practically smell the oil paints caked on her brush and staining her short nails. On that day, her blood had rushed from the high of creating her best paintings after months spent closed up in a friend's L.A. studio. She'd barely slept and hardly ate because the creative juices streaming through her system left little time or energy for anything other than her oils, brushes and canvases.

It had been the best time of her life, made possible only because of her roommate Sabrina's generosity. A fellow painter, Sabrina said she understood about the muse. She'd pressed the studio keys into Josie's palm and told her not to worry about rent for a few months. Josie hadn't thought twice about it. Sabrina said she was fat with trust fund money and promised she could afford to wait a few months for the back rent.

Then Sabrina had passed off Josie's artwork as her own and the L.A. art crowd bought the farce lock, stock and purloined brushstroke. When Josie had confronted Sabrina, she'd only laughed. Of course the artwork in her studio was hers. No one else was allowed to use the studio, everyone knew that.

Pushing back the anger, she berated herself. She should have known better than to let down her guard again.

Sam's hotel room door swung open and he strode out as naked as when she'd left him moments ago. "Where in the hell did you get this?" He brandished Rebecca's landscape treasure map, carelessly crumpling it in his right hand.

"Be careful with that! She did a great job capturing the light, that's not easy to do with charcoal."

"I don't give two shits about how well Rebecca captured the light. I want to know how in the hell you ended up with her stuff."

Through the angry red haze, the artist in her took in the strong lines of his profile and the shadow of a beard darkening his jawline. Her nipples stiffened as she recalled the warm taste of his hard abs when she'd licked her way across his six pack. She couldn't decide if she'd rather paint him or fuck him again. Probably both, but what she didn't want to do was fight him. Her nerves were too raw, and dammit, she didn't trust herself not to drag him back inside his room for some hard, fast, angry sex.

"Well, I hate to foil your plot to sleep with me for information but it's all a bunch of bullshit." He stalked toward her, his half-hard cock swinging in the breeze. "There's no treasure so it looks like you wasted your talents on me tonight."

Pompous ass. He didn't know a damn thing about her, but he sure was quick to think the worst. Battered pride steeled her spine. Let him think she'd slept with him only for some cockamamie treasure story, it was better than letting him realize the truth: that for a few hours he'd made her forget about everything else and made her feel like that princess who slew the dragon instead of the scullery maid always dashing around cleaning up everyone else's mess. Ha. That dragon was kicking her ass right now.

The elevator doors she'd been leaning against opened and Josie tumbled inside, landing on her ass.

Sam scowled down at her. "Serves you right."

"Maybe, but you're forgetting one thing." Josie couldn't contain the evil grin tightening her cheeks.

"What's that?"

"You're buck-ass naked and your room key is locked in your room."

His face turned scarlet and he cupped his large package in his equally big hands.

"See you never, shithead." The elevator doors slid shut and Josie stayed on the floor during the descent, nursing her wounded pride and an unfamiliar ache in her heart.

# Chapter Four

𝒥osie gagged on the stench of bacon grease heavy in the air at The Lucky Seven Diner. Head aching from a lack of sleep, she rubbed her scratchy eyes and dry-swallowed a pair of chalky aspirin tablets. What a way to start the second half of a double shift.

A quick glance at herself in the full-length mirror on the back of the employee break room door showed off red-rimmed eyes and violet crescents below. It looked as if she'd spent half the night crying—which she hadn't. A third of the night...maybe.

"Josie, three just sat down at table fifteen. It's yours." Arlene's voice, muffled by the closed door, bounced around her cranium like a pinball.

Time to make some money and save Cy's kneecaps even though her pain-in-the-ass little brother still hadn't returned any of her million or so messages. Desperate, she'd called the emergency number he'd given her a few months ago. A guy with a gruff voice took the message and promised he'd pass it along the next time he saw Cy, but he didn't say when that would be.

Why did everything have to go to shit at once?

She grabbed her order pad, stuffed a few pens in her apron and shuffled out of the break room. The early bird crowd filled most of the booths. If the seniors were here in force, that boded well for the drunk and disorderly customers who'd stumble in toward the end of her shift. Finally, some good luck.

Her step picked up a little bounce as she strode toward table fifteen and the weight on her shoulders lost a few pounds. On her way past the drink station, she swiped a silver carafe of coffee. Even at four in the afternoon, the early birders liked their coffee right away.

Josie whipped out a pen. "So, what'll you have?"

The words were barely out of her mouth when her heart stopped.

Sam sat flanked by a woman who looked like she'd gone twelve rounds in the octagon and the man from the poker game, whom she'd assumed was Sam's relative. Unlike her, Sam looked as though he'd spent the night undisturbed by what-ifs. Instead, he was all broad shoulders, golden hazel eyes and sex appeal. The bastard looked delicious.

Eventually, the shock wore off and her heart revived, beating so fast she felt the thrum in her ears and her body sizzled underneath her plain black T-shirt and ever-present jeans.

"Hey! I know you." The younger man broke the silence. "You were one of the waitresses at our poker game. That jerk sure did deserve it."

"Uh, thanks." She couldn't tear her gaze away from Sam and the way his ears turned pink, making her want to nibble on the lobes, right after she boxed them.

The man put his elbows on the table and leaned around Sam to get closer to the woman. "It was awesome. This asshole..." He glanced up at Josie. "Sorry about that. This jerk grabbed her tits..." He smiled an apology toward her. "Sorry. This jerk grabs her...breasts during the poker game. So, she takes this ginormous silver tray that she'd been using to carry the drinks and whacks him over the head with it. It was a sight to behold."

He relaxed back, a goofy grin on his face.

For his part, Sam had gone perfectly still. The sun streamed in from the window behind him, illuminating his light-brown hair and bringing out the auburn highlights. On another man, she'd assume those streaks had come from a stylist's talented hands, but not with Sam. No, he was too earthy for that. Not to mention she'd seen the touch of ginger down below. Her nipples hardened at the mental image, her body disregarding the do-not-want alert her brain telegraphed.

The woman's gaze flicked back and forth between Josie and Sam before she flipped up her heavy ceramic mug. "May I have some?"

Yanked out of her daze, Josie blinked a few times, trying to remember why she was here. "Uh, yeah."

"Josie," Sam's low voice rumbled.

His voice rolled over her like a protective blanket and for a second, she enjoyed the warmth—right up until the moment her pride fought through the comforting weight.

A tight smile pinched her cheeks and she jutted out her hip. "Do I know you?" She cocked her head to one side, sending her curls bouncing. "Oh yeah, you were at the poker game too, right? Scotch, neat, if I remember correctly."

"I..." Indecision wavered in his hazel eyes.

"You're hungry? Well, you came to the right place. Let me get your orders." Holding her pen at the ready, she turned toward the other guy. "What can I get you?"

After writing down their orders, Josie hurried back to the counter and cornered Arlene.

"Can you take table fifteen for me?"

"Thought you needed the tips?"

"Yeah, well, I'd rather gnaw off my own big toe than take any money from him."

Arlene smacked her wad of pale-pink gum. "Sure, I'll take 'em."

Anxious energy burned a hole through Josie's stomach as she marched past the order pick-up station and into the break room. The door's resounding thwack as she let it slam shut did little to relieve her aggression.

"I knew it. I just knew something was wrong. What happened?" Cy leaned against the opposite wall, his hands stuffed in his jeans pockets, an invisible aura of tightly wound energy filling the room.

Relief seeped into her bones. She'd really started to worry something had happened even though her twin alarm hadn't gone off. All the emotions of the past few days surged to the surface and she couldn't repress the tears making her blink or the sniffle that had her nose twitching. What was the point in hiding them? Cy always knew.

"Who is he? I have time to pay him a visit before leaving town."

At six-foot-five-inches tall, with each inch covered in muscle, her little brother could put the hurt on a man. But this time he was up against someone who brought a bazooka to a knife fight.

"It's Snips."

He made a gagging face. "Snips? That's disgusting. What were you thinking?"

Men. Of course that's where his brain went first.

"I didn't fuck him, Mr. All Brawn No Brains. He's forcing forty thousand dollars out of me that he says you owe him—money I don't have, by the way. So why don't you tell me what in the hell you were thinking?"

Cy shoved his fingers through his platinum hair, still cut short from his time in a hush-hush Marine unit. "Shit. I was hoping it wouldn't come to this."

"Come to what?"

He grabbed her backpack from its hook and strutted over, dropping the bag at her feet. "You have to leave town. Now."

"Hey, I would be if I didn't have Snips hounding me to pay your debt or he'll get the cash from Mom and Dad. You know they don't have any money."

"Mom and Dad are safe. I moved them to Lake Havasu last night. A buddy worked it so Dad got hired on with a plumbing crew there. Mom's a block away from a dialysis-care unit."

The twin-thing went on full alert and a jolt of electricity charged down her spine. "Cy, you better tell me what's going on. Now."

He crossed his arms over his wide chest and hit her with his best menacing glare, but said nothing.

"Look, I know you supposedly can kill me with only your thumb, but stop trying to scare me into shutting up. It won't work." Josie jabbed her finger into the middle of his hard chest. "Spill it."

He ground his teeth. "Snips is working his way up the chain of command and thinks that bringing me to the Callandriello capos will get him promoted even faster."

"No offense, Cy, 'cuz you know I love you, but how does you owing forty K give him more influence?"

"I don't owe Snips a penny. The bastard is trying to flush me out and using you to do it. The Callandriellos want me because they have a hit out on the governor's daughter and I'm the one keeping her alive. You didn't really think I left the Corps to do odd jobs, did you?"

Little incongruities suddenly made sense. The travel. Cy being out of touch so much. The standoffish way he treated her whenever she asked what was going on in his life. "Thank God, I was worried you were gambling again. So who do you work for?"

"That's not important."

She flayed him with a dirty look.

Cy took a step back. "I'd tell you if I could, but I can't. All you need to know is that I'm with the good guys and that you need to get the hell out of Vegas."

"What do I do about Snips?"

"Don't worry about him. I'll take care of it."

"I'm supposed to go to Nebraska and stay at the Rose O'Neill Dry Creek Artist Colony for six months, but how do I do that if you're in trouble?"

"What's wrong, pussycat, you think I can't take care of little ol' me?" He flexed his pecs and winked. "Get your ass to Dry Creek and lay low. I wouldn't put it past Snips to try to use you as bait again if he finds you. I'll check in on you, but Nebraska is one of the last places anyone would ever look. Hell, I don't think most people could find it on a map."

She rolled her eyes. "Cy, is all of this really necessary? It's Snips. He's a wannabe."

"He's a scumbag with major ambition to be somebody. How soon can you get to Nebraska?"

"I'll leave after I get off work."

"Do it. Don't call Mom or Dad after you leave. I have someone watching the 'rents, but I wouldn't put it past that little prick to find a way to tap into their phones. Here, take this." He handed her a cheap cellphone. "It's a pay-as-you-go phone. Untraceable. Leave your cell in Vegas so they can't track the GPS chip and take this one with you to Nebraska. I have the number already. Don't give it to anyone else."

Josie rubbed her arms, which prickled with goose bumps. "Fuck. Now you're starting to scare me."

"Good." Cy's eyes, the same shade of gray as hers, went dark. "You *should* be scared."

They hugged, his sinewy arms squeezing the air out of her lungs. Damn, he hadn't done that since before he'd left for overseas.

"Be safe, little bro."

He grinned down at her. "If you haven't noticed, I'm not that little. Talk to you soon." With that, he strutted out the back door.

Cy had saved her back in L.A., bought her first canvas after that debacle and urged her to paint again. He knew, had always known, how important painting was to her sanity. They'd always had each other's backs before, so there was no reason to think this time would be any different.

Josie stepped back out among the diner's tables. Other waitresses buzzed around, dropping off food and pouring coffee. Customer chatter filled the room as if everything in the world was normal, as if she hadn't just discovered her brother was some sort of covert operative working for God knows who and a

Avery Flynn

loan shark with delusions of grandeur was trying to use her as bait.

Desperate to stay busy, she snagged a stack of napkins along with the bucket of loose silverware and headed toward a table to roll the cheap forks, spoons and knives inside the paper napkins. The mindless work would help bring her heart rate back to normal.

"You better have my money."

A squeak escaped and she spun around.

Snips lounged at the table closest to the employee-only door, usually reserved for busboys scarfing down roast beef sandwiches during break. He wore a gray track suit, a black newsboy cap pulled low over his forehead and sunglasses, presumably to hide evidence of what had to be a gnarly bruise. The whole ensemble made him look like a cheap imitation of the type of people Vegas had in surplus.

Seeing him pissed her off. The little fuck had stirred up all this trouble. It took everything she had not to punch him in the face, but what he lacked in style he made up for with a short-fuse temper and deadly aim.

He smirked at her. "Cy is still avoiding my calls. I can't have that. My rep demands fast action."

Willing herself not to smack him over the head again with any of the tools of her trade, she took a deep breath and counted to ten. She couldn't let on that she knew the debt was a ruse. Cy needed time to put some distance between him and this power-hungry little shit.

"Look, Snips —"

"Nobody calls me that anymore. It's Jimmy now." His cheeks flushed.

People had called him Snips since freshman year when he showed up for yearbook picture day with a completely jacked-up home haircut. Even back then he'd been a shithead, but he hadn't had the paid muscle to back up his flapping gums.

Not so today. Linc, the giant sitting across from him, cracked his scraped knuckles.

Josie had to play it just right. Until she skipped town, he had to believe she was getting him the money.

"Fine. Jimmy, let's do this logically. Cy owes you forty grand. I have ten I can have to you as soon as the bank opens tomorrow. I'll have the rest for you in a month."

"Oh yeah, how's that gonna happen?"

"I have a line on something."

Snips looked at his goon and cocked his head toward Josie. "Sounds just like her no-nuts brother, doesn't she?"

Josie dug her fingernails into her palm to keep from snapping back at him. "If you'll just hear me out—"

"Unless you have the full forty K, the only offer I want to hear from you involves you naked and bent over."

A shadow fell over the table and a hand landed on her shoulder, yanking her back.

"That's no way to talk to a lady unless you're not too fond of your teeth." Sam angled his body so he stood between her and Snips.

"Who the fuck are you?" The no-neck monster lumbered up from his seat to his full height, towering over Sam, who, at six feet, wasn't exactly a shrimp.

"I'm the guy who's about to teach you two some manners." Sam puffed his chest out and took a step forward. "Who wants the first lesson?"

This would not turn out well. As pissed as she was at Sam, she didn't want him to end up with a permanent limp because of his misplaced sense of propriety. She whipped around her self-appointed knight and found herself nose-to-sternum with Snips' goon.

"Everybody calm down." She jutted her butt out, pushing Sam back a few paces. "This is not the time or the place for a testosterone smack down. The last thing I need is to lose this job too."

"Josie—"

"Can it, Sam." She leveled at glare at Snips and his smarmy grin. "And you aren't going to get *any* money if I don't have a job. So everybody chill out."

Frustration vibrated off of Sam, pummeling her with its intensity. Without thinking about the reason why, she twisted her fingers between his and held tight. He returned her squeeze and together they stared down Snips and his enforcer until the loan shark shrugged as if their wall of defiance wasn't worth getting upset over.

"Whatever." Snips stood up and adjusted the collar of his track suit, sticking out his pinky finger so the gold ring on it glinted. "I'll be in touch, Josie. You better come up with some cash fast."

"I'll get it."

"Good, I'd hate to have to go convince your mom to hock her wheelchair, because that's the only thing of value your parents have."

"Leave them out of this."

"Get my money or they'll be my next stop." He pushed past her, knocking his shoulder against Sam as he went by. "And if I ever see you again, the scar I'll give you will look like King Kong next to that little scratch on your ugly mug."

"You're welcome to try." The promise of violence lay thick in Sam's retort.

Heart in her throat, Josie watched Snips and his muscle mosey out of the dinner.

"Nice friends."

She snorted. "Friend is not the word for Snips Esposito." Josie looked up at Sam, his face so close to hers. "Why did you do that?"

"Do what?"

"Help."

His gaze dropped to her princess tattoo and he brushed a finger across the bright-red dragon tail, a strange, sad smile curving his lips.

Her entire body went on alert, desperate for another touch even as her mind warned her to run away.

He crushed his lips to hers, coaxing them open with his tongue and claiming her mouth like a conquering hero.

Josie curled her fingers into the hair at the nape of his neck, as soft and pliant as the rest of him was hard and demanding, and kissed him back. The air crackled around them as fire spread through her body, burning hottest at her core.

Sam broke the kiss. "The better question is why I did *that*."

Chest heaving, he slid his thumb across her kiss-swollen bottom lip then turned and strode out of the restaurant.

# Chapter Five

*H*owling gusts molded last night's six-inch snowfall into mini-mountains outside Josie's studio window. She exhaled a deep breath onto the cold glass and drew a quick profile into the resulting fog. A proud, straight nose. A square jar set in a stubborn line. A scar slashed across a high cheekbone. Her subconscious had pushed the same face onto every canvas since she'd arrived in Dry Creek.

Forty-two days of nothing but painting with minimal stops for sleeping or eating should have been heaven. Instead, the forced solitude felt more like hell. She'd alternated between fits of frantic creativity, attacking the canvas with bright hues of yellow and orange, to days of boiling frustration as the blank square taunted her.

In normal circumstances she would have gone for a run or escaped into a dark movie theater. Great ideas always seemed to come during such downtime. But her days hadn't been normal since Snips lied about her brother's debt and she had to go into pseudo-seclusion. So she prowled her isolated cabin like a chained dog, discontent choking off her inspiration.

Cy called to check in several times, ending every conversation with a warning to stay to herself. Like that would be a problem. Winter was the quiet season at the Rose O'Neill Dry Creek Artist Colony. Twenty artists had lived in the individual studio cabins on the south edge of Dry Creek when she'd arrived. Now, only herself and owner Celestine Arthur remained—oh, and her stubborn imagination's version of Sam Layton. His hazel eyes stared at her from the dozens of abandoned canvases scattered around the room.

"Get out of my head, you bastard." Josie swiped his profile off the glass with the palm of her hand, the window's cold icing her palm.

"You need to find yourself a boy toy."

Josie started and spun around.

Celestine slammed the cabin's front door closed behind her. Clumps of snow dropped from her boots as the woman stomped on the rug. "I'd alway meant to tell Bruce the cabins needed small porches but damn, I'd take one look at him shirtless and sweaty, whacking away with that big ol' hammer of his, and forget what in the hell I'd meant to tell him. Worst carpenter and best nude model I ever had here."

The older woman's angular, liver-spotted face softened for a moment. The corners of her chapped lips curled ever so slightly upward. Then she blinked. The softness melted away into her normal hard look that made you wonder if she ate nails or prunes for breakfast. In a movie, her crusty exterior would have hidden a heart of gold. But after a month and a half of chipping away at Celestine's hard exterior, Josie had only revealed more crust.

"Sure, come on in." Josie softened the words with a smile, glad for the company. It wasn't as if she'd been all soft and gushy herself lately. Maybe that's why they got along so well.

"Oh, we've gotten past the knocking stage, didn't you know?" Celestine picked up a half-finished painting from where it leaned against the wall. "I see you've painted Sam Layton again. That mother of his is a real piece of work. I wouldn't go near any of her boys if I was you."

Mile-deep frown lines creased her forehead as she gave Josie a long head-to-toe perusal.

"There are plenty of strapping men in Dry Creek. You swing that high butt of yours at them at Robidoux's Roadhouse, they'll come swarming and you'll have your pick of any non-Layton in the county."

Josie kept her mouth shut. It wasn't the first time they'd had this particular conversation. Odds were it wouldn't be the last because she had no intention of following the older woman's advice. The last thing in the world she needed was a man between her legs. Just the memory of the disastrous night with Sam in Vegas made her palms clammy and her cheeks flush with embarrassment and regret. The mere idea of repeating the experience held no appeal.

Celestine poked through Josie's work, something she did every day, mumbling under her breath and leaving small puddles of melted snow on the floor as she walked. She stood silent for several minutes with her head cocked to the left in front of Josie's latest attempt. Vivid reds and yellows swirled together, blending into thick orange flames as a man, who looked suspiciously like the world's hottest history professor, gazed out at the horizon.

"You've got talent," Celestine grumbled as she turned to face Josie. "Just need to get that man out of your head. Best way to do that is to get a new one in your bed."

The woman was like a dog with a pork chop with this particular topic. "I have enough going on in my life without any new complications."

"It's only complicated if you make it. You need to unscrew the pressure valve if you want to actually finish one of these. I'm old and pissed off most of the time, but even I like to get out and have some fun once in a while. You should try it."

Josie rolled her eyes. "Yeah, but your version of fun is putting people on edge wondering what's going to come out of your mouth next."

This time Celestine's smile deepened to show a dimple in her left cheek. "True, but before the arthritis made my knees ache, I loved to dance. You ever two-stepped?"

"I don't even know what that is."

"Well, then I suggest you get yourself down to Robidoux's Roadhouse and find out." Celestine clomped over to the front door, shoved a hand deep inside a pocket and pulled out a set of keys that she deposited on the window ledge. "Take my truck. The tires on your bucket of bolts are for crap and I don't want to have to come tow you out of the ditch at three in the morning."

With that, she disappeared out the door.

Josie eyeballed the set of keys and shook her head ruefully. Maybe Celestine had a heart after all.

She stepped toward the window, but her body protested with bone-deep aches and a twitching shoulder muscle. She surrendered to the inevitable, pivoted and made her way down the short hall to her bedroom, fully planning to pass out without changing. Her eyes were narrow slits when she flopped down on the bed, landing on top of a hard lump. Josie slid her hand beneath her body, grasped the offending object, then yanked out Rebecca's diary.

Rebecca had become her three o'clock in the morning companion, distracting her from thoughts about her one night with Sam. At first she'd cracked open the leather binding expecting to be bored into slumber. Instead, the diary sucked Josie in. That poor woman. Josie thought *she'd* had it bad, but at least she wasn't stuck crossing the country in a covered wagon.

Rebecca had started her journey full of hope and excitement. She and her twenty-year-old spinster aunt had snuck out of her parents' home on a moonless night, determined to travel to Oregon where her true love waited for her. She'd made it as far as Dry Creek when she'd learned her John had died. That had been a three-tissue entry for sure.

Eyeing the leather-bound book through cracked eyelids, Josie rolled onto her back. She'd read most of it during the past week. Only a few pages remained. Curiosity propped her weary eyes open. She'd read the last few passages then go to sleep.

*August 30, 1865*

*I have decided not to carry on with this journey. There is a town nearby and the land here welcomes me. It is a vast open space, but there is a stark beauty that speaks to my loneliness. Aunt Abigail tells me I am too deep in my own grief for such a decision, but I know it is the correct one. I have more than enough gold pieces to buy a small plot of land, the hired man, Mr. Harrison, has agreed to stay on. I do believe he did so only to remain near Abigail, but I dare not ask either of them outright. The emerald earbobs and other jewelry I sewed into my clothes have limited value here, as this is not a place where jewels are seen or celebrated. After the decadent displays of my parents' home, that is a relief. In jest, I told Abigail I would bury them. This scandalized her, of course.*

*September 29, 1865*

*We have purchased a plot near a tower of rock they call McPherson's Bluff. Our acreage lies in its shadow. The days are filled with far too much work to play, but I find myself sketching the bluff by the light of the evening fire. Abigail and I are determined to make a go of our little farm. My mother would look askance at the blisters on my hands. She had such hopes that I would follow in her footsteps and marry a man of a certain standing. My dearly departed John did not meet her requirement. Even though all has not happened as I planned when Abigail and I departed from St. Louis, I do not regret my choices. My mother had despaired of ever making a lady of me. I had despaired of what would happen if she succeeded.*

*October 15, 1865*

*Mr. Franklin Layton paid a call today. He owns a ranch nearby. I could tell from his eyes that he is a kind man. They are a green-brown color with gold flecks. He is not John, but a good man. I told him I would look forward to his next visit.*

*November 30, 1865*

*Franklin comes to court nearly every day now. Abigail wonders when he ever tends to his cattle with the amount of time he spends here. I wonder how I manage not to expire while he is gone. I know when he approaches long before I see the dust his horse kicks up as he crosses the prairie. When we walk together I fear my heart will burst from my chest. My dearly departed John will always be a part of me, however I do believe Franklin is my future happiness. He is a man who is a part of this place. Strong and brave. He stands against the winds that never stop blowing and challenges the elements to stop him. My heart weeps each time he leaves to return to his ranch.*

*December 23, 1865*

*So it is done. I have buried my past, forgotten the large house in St. Louis and tomorrow will become Mrs. Franklin Layton. The weather cleared today as if Providence smiled upon us. Though the air was quite cold, I walked along McPherson's Bluff, its limestone walls familiar to me now. Here is where I said goodbye to all I was and greeted my new beginning. This shall be my final entry in this diary.*

Josie traced her finger across Rebecca's ornate script with its curves and curls. She could picture a small farmhouse out in the flat plain. Okay, her vision looked a lot like *Little House on the Prairie*, but she doubted she was that far off base. What a life Rebecca had lived. The treasure Saul had spoken of had to be the emerald earrings and other jewelry she'd sewn into her garments. They must be worth a small fortune.

Her head sank farther down into the fluffy pillows. In the dark behind her eyelids, a face came to light; an all-too-familiar face with hazel eyes that reminded her of a tiger on the prowl. And he was after her. Heat pooled in her belly as the man in her imagination stalked closer, naked from the waist up. Her nipples stiffened. His long fingers found the button of his jeans and flicked it open. In her mind, Josie urged him on, practically begging him to lower the denim from his lean hips. He hooked his thumb in his waistband and—

Damn it, Celestine was right. She needed to get the hell out of this cabin and force Sam out of her head.

Twenty minutes later, she pounded the fat pillow for the hundredth time, trying to mold the feathers and her lustful thoughts into submission. But she couldn't vanquish visions of Sam's burnt-sienna locks between her thighs as his tongue twisted a figure eight around her clit.

Might as well just go with what her body wanted.

Sliding her fingers under the waistband of her panties, her mind replaced her fingers with Sam's. Slowly, she traced the path he'd taken, remembering the feel of his firm tongue on her most tender of spots. With all the foreplay her imagination had put her through, it didn't take long before vibrations started in her core and spread to her thighs. Almost before she was ready, her body tensed and her climax lifted her shoulders off the bed and arched her spine.

The thundering on her door evaporated her post-orgasm bliss. The clock read 1:13. Her heart rate sped up for a much less sexually satisfying reason. No good ever came from visitors at this hour. She yanked up her pants then sprinted to the door, unlocked it and whipped it open.

"'Bout damn time. It's colder than a witch's tit out here." Celestine marched in and shoved a cordless phone toward Josie. "You got a call."

Her heart hiccuped in her chest. The black plastic rectangle transformed from a communication device into the harbinger of doom.

"What are you waiting for, me to hold it up to your ear? He said it was important."

God, what if Snips had found Cy? Or their parents? Panic grabbed ahold of her throat and squeezed tight. *Stop being such a fucking chicken and take the stupid phone.*

Clamping down on the last bit of calm she had, Josie grabbed the phone and held its icy receiver to her ear. "Cy?"

"You wish, you little bitch." Snips' voice lashed her as cruelly as a whip. "That Saul sure is a chatty old guy, nearly talked my ear off tonight. How's Dry Creek, Nebraska?"

Her stomach sank but his words buoyed her spirits. If he was talking to her, that meant he hadn't found Cy. "It was better five minutes ago."

"That smart mouth is going to get you in trouble one of these days."

"So I've been told." Taking a deep breath, she steadied herself to sell the lie. "Look, I'll get you the money."

"Can the bullshit, I heard all about your brother's secret visit to the diner. Not all of the waitresses there are as snooty as you."

Josie bit her bottom lip in surprise and every ounce of badass attitude deserted her. She stared at the knot in the oak doorframe and waited, breathless, for the other shoe to drop.

"We both know he doesn't owe me a dime. But now *you* do."

The raw arrogance in Snips' voice brought her spirit back to life. "What the hell for?"

"Getting in the way, bitch."

"You're out of your mind."

"Saul told me all about Rebecca's Bounty. I want that treasure. All of it. You want to live. Fuck up, and

64

I'll hand over you and Cy half dead to Callandriello so the big man can finish the job himself. It'll be worth finding your asshole brother just for that. But first, I'd make a quick stop in Lake Havasu to pay a call on your parents. OH yes, your parents' next door neighbors were quite chatty with the right motivation. Normally, that would be Linc's job, but I think I'd really enjoy delivering the message to your mom and dad."

"No." Anxiety twisted her muscles into a pretzel. How had he found her parents' hiding spot? It didn't matter. What mattered was protecting her parents. "I'll do it."

"You have a week. Linc will be in touch." He paused. "And don't go telling your brother or anyone else about this. If I even suspect you're looking to double-cross me, I'll be at your parents' front door faster than greyhounds at the dog track. Got it?"

"Yeah," she whispered, defeated.

"Good."

The dial tone blared in her ear, but her brain was too overwhelmed to send the correct signal to her body to hand the phone back to Celestine.

"You okay there?" Concern crinkled the middle of the older woman's already wrinkled forehead and she pried the phone from Josie's death grip.

"Fine," she mumbled as she herded Celestine out the door. "Goodnight."

As soon as the door shut, Josie swiped a paintbrush and twirled it between her fingers. She paced the small studio floor, dodging half-finished canvases and rags covered in oil paint. She didn't know how to get ahold of Cy. The emergency number he'd given her wasn't a direct line, so she could only leave a message. Their parents couldn't protect themselves from Snips' fury. She had to find the treasure.

Stopping in front of a half-finished painting, she stared at the man who had haunted her subconscious since Vegas. Having the diary alone wouldn't be enough to find the treasure and save her parents. The map was the key—and Sam had the map.

# Chapter Six

*A*bout a month ago, while driving down Main Street, Sam had caught a flash of white-blonde hair. He'd done such a fast double take he'd nearly broken his neck, but the woman had disappeared. Since then he couldn't shake Josie's ghost.

He scanned the mostly female students in front of him in Cather College's biggest lecture hall. There were dishwater blondes, bleached blondes, wheat blondes and strawberry blondes, but no one with the right shade of platinum.

Heat flushed his cheeks as soon as he realized he was doing it again. Searching for her. He chewed the inside of his cheek, disgusted with his own flight of fancy, and glanced at his notes.

"So the author argues that Amelia Earhart served as a kind of tie between the post-suffrage time period and the modern feminism movement of the 1960s." Sam swiped down his touchscreen tablet on the lectern, scrolling for the appropriate citation, but the clang of a metal door drew his attention to the back of the lecture hall.

Josie stood by the door, one hip cocked. Her shock of white-blonde hair bounced around her face in curls that touched the collar of her black leather jacket. Black boots encased her long legs to mid-thigh. His gaze traveled over the rest of her leather-covered curves, past her full red lips to her big gray eyes. She looked as if she'd just walked off a movie set and she was playing badass heroine number one, albeit with dusky shadows under her eyes.

Her steel gaze met his and she shrugged as if in apology for the noise.

"Adventure is worthwhile in itself." The quote came out unbidden and again he tasted the sweetness of her wrist where the words were tattooed.

She quirked an eyebrow and winked before sliding into an empty seat in the back row.

Everything became silent as the students, who had been clacking away on their laptops, stilled. His lecture escaped him. Something about Amelia Earhart, feminism and Midwestern women.

He should be more ticked off that Josie had turned up out of the blue, disturbing his peace of mind and invading his lecture hall. Her appearance only confirmed that she was just another treasure hunter. Vegas had been a setup. All she wanted was to dig up Rebecca's Bounty. A flicker of annoyance burned in his gut, but he couldn't fan it into a full fury.

Even if it hadn't meant anything to her, that night had opened up a part of Sam that he'd thought he'd lost years ago. Suddenly, the rigidity of his life chafed. He yearned to challenge Dry Creek's perception of him as the quiet Layton. The tragic Layton. Josie may not have gotten what she'd wanted out of him in Vegas, but he sure as hell had gotten a completely unexpected gift—a second chance of sorts. If he could break out of his comfort zone and go for it.

Then she licked her pouty lips with that pink tongue of hers and all rational thought fled. All he could think about was the amber scent of her creamy skin and the way she'd swirled her hips when he'd buried himself deep inside her.

The memory forced him to shift uncomfortably. Suddenly he was very thankful the lectern stood tall enough to block the view of his stiffening cock. His mouth dried as if he'd eaten six pounds of cotton. Seventy pairs of eyes stared, but only the laughing gray eyes in the back row held his interest. He fidgeted with his tablet, buying time to gather his thoughts and forget the woman who'd been dogging him in his dreams and fantasies.

Josie unzipped her jacket, revealing a low-cut emerald sweater that displayed mountains of cleavage.

What had been a vague sense of discomfort morphed into an urgent need to touch her soft skin again.

"Dr. Layton?"

Sam glanced down at a student in the front row.

The girl's brow wrinkled with concern.

*Pull it together, moron.* "Yes, sorry about that. My notes seem to have, uh, disappeared, so let's call it a day, everyone. See you on Wednesday."

He stayed glued to his spot behind the lectern while the students filed out of the lecture hall. Their chatter covered the tension stretching between him and Josie, but once they were gone there was nothing left to diffuse it. Need slammed into him even as he acknowledged she only wanted to use him because he had Rebecca's map. But unlike the bombshell goddess heading his way, who had probably never heard the word no, he knew the difference between needing, wanting and getting. She was about to learn. Then she'd leave him alone and he would stop thinking of her at odd moments of the day. And all through the night.

"Long time no chat, Sam." She strutted down the stairs. "How've you been?"

"I'm not going to help you." He dropped his eyes to his briefcase and shoved everything inside, forgetting his natural orderly process in his haste to get away from Josie and the temptations she offered.

Her Ferrari red lips curled and she paused at the bottom of the stairs. "Help with what?"

His fingers curled around the edge of the lectern and he tried to block out her warm scent taunting him. "Rebecca's Bounty."

"What makes you think the treasure is why I'm here?" She closed the distance between them, stopping just out of his reach.

"Please, don't insult my intelligence."

She shrugged. "Fine, it's true. But that's not the only reason why I'm here."

"Oh yeah, is this where you tell me some cock-and-bull story about how you've been dreaming of me every night?"

She leaned forward, her breasts threatening to spill out of her sweater. "Sounds to me like you're projecting. Is there something keeping *you* up at night?"

Sam kept his mouth shut. He'd already said enough.

Josie reached inside her jacket and brought out a small leather book. "A peace offering."

When he didn't say anything, she placed the book on the lectern, her fingers brushing his, sending an electric jolt of a reminder of just how much he wanted this confounding woman.

"It's Rebecca's diary. I thought it should be back with your family."

That threw him for a loop. "What's the catch?"

She sidled up to him, her breathing shallow. "No catch, but the treasure is out there. I have a pretty good idea of the general location. If we work together, using your map, I know we'll find it."

He chuckled. "Do you know how many people have searched for that treasure and for how long?" Including himself. "What makes you think you'll be the one to find it?" He locked his briefcase and moved toward the door.

"Don't you ever go by faith, by gut feeling?"

He stilled at the challenge in her alto voice. Brash and defiant, she was an Amazon who couldn't be controlled. He was a college professor who ironed his T-shirts and micromanaged everything in his world. He shouldn't want her, but, dammit, he couldn't stop.

His stomach cramped at the idea of working with her and not succumbing to his desire. "No."

"What happened to you, Sam? You're different, less adventurous than you were in Vegas."

Las Vegas had been an aberration, an anomaly. Here in Dry Creek, that easygoing Sam didn't exist, hadn't for a very long time.

"This is the real me, Josie." He faced her. "No lies."

"Don't insult *my* intelligence now, Sam. You're not thinking clearly. Think of what we could find. A piece of your family's history."

Damn it, how did she know just what buttons to push? But little did she realize his reasons for seeking Rebecca's Bounty over the past two decades had nothing to do with finding a piece of history and everything to do with Michael. If she was right, he could finally deliver on the promise he'd made to a dying boy. He grit his teeth, hoping she wouldn't see the cracks in his armor.

"So what do you get out of this, Josie?"

A trio of students barged into the room, talking loudly. They sat down in the back and pulled out laptops from their bags.

He glanced at the clock. Professor Schaffer's lecture would begin in about ten minutes. He grabbed Josie's hand, pulling her to the exit. "Come on, we can talk in my office."

"Yes, sir." She gave him an awkward left-handed salute since he was holding her right.

They emerged into the bright January sunlight, the glare glinting off the hard-packed snow covering the Cather College quad. A frigid blast of air swept across the open space and Josie shivered beside him before zipping up her leather jacket. It was perfect for a Vegas winter, but a pitiful excuse for a winter coat in Nebraska.

He glanced down at her boots. Not surprisingly, they weren't made for walking on ice. The damn things had such spindly heels that he couldn't imagine how she walked in them period. He didn't want her to fall on the slick brick walkway, that's why he didn't let go of her hand. Why else would he pull her closer to his side other than to help block the wind from freezing her solid?

Sam ignored the little voice laughing inside his head and quickened his pace, keeping time with the chattering of her teeth. A few minutes later, he turned toward Sandoz Hall and the warmth of his cramped office. He'd make some coffee; that would warm her up. Not that he cared. It was just common courtesy, that's all.

"Are we close?" Her teeth chattered.

"Yep, that building up ahead."

At that moment, he spotted the telltale neon-green winter coat and matching bedazzled knit hat. Only one human being in the world thought neon green needed to be jazzed up.

Mom.

Luckily, Glenda Layton's back was to them as she walked toward his office. Shit. If his mother saw them together, she wouldn't rest until she knew everything about Josie. And when it came to digging up gossip, no one was better than his mother—especially if it involved her children. Persuading Glenda not to interfere in her children's lives was about as easy as teaching a goat to use a fork and knife.

Glenda stopped in the middle of the sidewalk, her gloved hand digging through her purse. She brought out a cellphone.

"Yellow," she hollered into the phone, her mispronounced greeting carrying over the wind.

If he played it right, he could get past her. Gripping Josie's ice-cold fingers in his, he sped up the pace.

Swerving around the students shuffling to class, he hoped a few of the wrapped-up co-eds would serve as a wall between them and Glenda. Ignoring Josie's squawk of protest, he hoofed it down the sidewalk.

A few feet now and they'd be past Glenda and her inquiring mind.

Right as they were steps away from his mom, she snapped the phone shut and turned.

He and Josie came face-to-face with Glenda.

She took in the otherworldly blonde beside him and her gaze traveled down to his fingers wrapped around Josie's. When she looked back up, he swore he could see grandchildren reflected in the depths of her brown eyes.

Before she could open her mouth, he blurted out the first thing to come to mind. "Hi, Mom! Big meeting, talk to you later."

Yanking Josie along, he sped toward his office, knowing he'd only postponed the inevitable.

"Shit, we're not going to make it in time." Josie jerked to a halt.

"What?"

The appearance of the thug from the Vegas diner answered one question and created so many more.

# Chapter Seven

$\mathcal{J}$osie's stomach sank to her toes.

"Where you going in such a hurry?" Linc cracked his knuckles.

"Inside where it's warm." She hoped he'd chalk up her shivers to the weather instead of the bone-deep fear making her spasm.

Linc stuck out his chest. He didn't bother to look at her, but locked his gaze on Sam. "Got a message for you from Mr. Esposito."

"What, Snips can't pick up the phone again?" She shivered but refused to give up any ground.

That earned her a look from the giant, who looked even bigger in a puffy coat. Who'd have thought it was possible? The guy was six feet seven and a wall of solid muscle. There were buildings on Dry Creek's Main Street that cast a smaller shadow.

"I'd hate to have to tell him you called him that, considering all he's done to accommodate your special circumstances."

She rolled her eyes. "Yeah right. He wants..." She swallowed back the truth. "What he wants."

Linc returned his attention to Sam. "Why don't you take a walk so the lady and I can talk business."

Sam took a menacing step forward, half blocking her from Linc's view. "Why don't you go—"

"Sam!" Josie wasn't cold anymore even though her breath hung in the cold air like a cumulous cloud. She stepped around him and sent him a pleading look. Even as solid as Sam felt beside her, Linc made his living hurting people. "Please, I can take care of this."

The tension in his shoulders screamed out how much he wanted to object, but he pursed his lips together and shot Linc a die-scum look instead.

The big man's face lost all expression and icy dread filled her up so fully she feared her bones might crack.

"Mr. Esposito wants to make sure you really understand what you've got riding on this." He held out a photo of an adobe ranch-style house. Her mother sat in her wheelchair on the porch.

Anxiety curled around her brainstem and she battled her dueling instincts of attacking Linc or running away.

"Leave my parents out of this." She barely heard her own words over the blood rushing in her ears.

Her choices were nil. She had to trick Sam into helping her find the treasure, steal it from under his nose and give it up to that shithead Snips. Only then would her parents be safe. It wasn't fair. It wasn't right. But it was the only way out of this mess for her family.

"Why don't you just get the fuck out of here, or do I have to make you?" Sam snarled the question.

Josie whipped around, taking in the firm set to Sam's jaw and the way his hands curled into fists at his sides. "Stay out of this, Sam."

The giant's smirk practically shouted out his hope that Sam would take a swing. "Don't fuck this up, Josie, or it won't just be you and Cyril facing the consequences."

He walked away, a crowd of students parting automatically to make room for him, as if they knew that evil walked amongst them and wanted to get as far away as possible.

❧❧❧

It took thirty seconds before Josie could feel the tips of her ears and another fifteen before her earlobes began to throb as the blood vessels opened up in reaction to the warmth of Sam's office. Linc had to have already been in Dry Creek when that bastard Snips called in the wee hours this morning. He wasn't leaving anything to chance. Neither could she.

"Sam—"

He silenced her by holding up his hand. "First things first."

Ignoring her, he busied himself with a single-cup coffee maker on a sideboard that wouldn't dare hold a speck of dust, if the rest of Sam's office was anything to go by. The bookshelf by a large window held books alphabetized by author. The pen cup on his desk held only black pens. A white, unlined notepad sat near the phone. The rest of his desk was as barren as Nebraska looked from 20,000 feet above.

The only bit of color came in the form of the lone framed photo on the bookshelf. In it, Sam, three other men and a woman towered over a younger redheaded woman with curly hair and a devil-may-care smirk. Josie picked it up for a closer look. One of the men had been with Sam in Vegas. Must be a brother. The other men she didn't recognize, but the deep laugh lines and bald head of the tallest identified him as Dad. The tall woman, his mother that they'd passed on the sidewalk, had Sam's serious face. Her fierceness was undiminished by the ornery side-eye glance she leveled at the father.

"The Laytons." He stood behind her, casting a shadow over the family photo.

She tried to ignore it, but a frisson of something buzzed between them, sweeping against her skin and overheating her flesh until her thin sweater felt as if it was made of thick Irish wool. She shrugged out of her jacket, laughing inside as his gaze dipped lower and then snapped back up to her eyes a millisecond later.

"Your mom looks like a handful."

"You have no idea." He handed her a plain white mug filled with coffee.

"Thank you."

"Have a seat." He nodded toward an empty wooden chair across from his perfectly clean desk.

She sat down and Sam lounged against one corner of the desk.

She had to ignore the way the light played in his hair, the hint of promise in his eyes and the way he always appeared in her paintings. Sam was a means to an end—to save her parents from Snips' vengeance. She had to remember that, no matter how much she wished it wasn't the truth.

"I need your help finding the treasure." Not her smoothest request, but she had to get the words out before the guilt twisting her gut overwhelmed her family-preservation instincts.

"Tell me what the hell this is all about. Who is Snips and why is he threatening your parents?"

"I can't tell you that."

Sam grabbed her arm, sending another spark of awareness skittering up her skin. "I need to know what the hell the urgency is all about on your part. What's the real threat?"

Her spine stiffened. "None of your damn business. Let go of me now."

His gaze dropped to his fingers wrapped around her upper arm and a flush crept into his cheeks. He let go and stepped back as if burned. "Sorry, I shouldn't have touched you."

An awkward silence filled the room, pushing the tension higher.

She couldn't tell him the truth. The less he knew, the easier it would be to take what she had to and walk away. A pang of regret clanged in her belly, but she turned a deaf ear to her conscience. If waitressing had taught her anything, it was how to spin a tale that paralleled the truth as closely as possible to get the customer on her side. If it worked for a messed-up drink order, she'd make it work for something much more important—her parents' lives.

Ignoring the unease burbling in her gut, she pressed forward. "Forty thousand."

"What?" Those hazel eyes of his rounded in surprise.

"My brother, Cy, owes his loan shark, Snips, forty K for a can't-miss business opportunity that did. Snips can't find Cy, but still wants his money." The words tumbled out, burying her in deceit. "When I read Rebecca's diary, I realized the treasure is real. She buried something—probably jewelry."

"People have been hunting for Rebecca's Bounty for longer than I've been alive." His tone turned harsh and dark, pain bleeding through despite his attempt to hide it. "They've found maps in the past, all of which were exposed as fakes. Can't you come up with the money another way?"

Josie snorted. "I've already emptied my lavish savings account and been turned down for a personal loan from every bank in Vegas that doesn't do business with a baseball bat. My dad's been out of work for months, but finally found a job with the friend of a friend in Arizona. My mom needs dialysis several times a week and is on disability. If Snips goes after them, it won't be pretty."

"Your brother sounds like a real winner."

Her protective instincts perked up. "Hey, he's a good guy. Mostly. He'd been in trouble in the past, but Cy cleaned up his act a few years ago."

"So where is he now?"

Her brain went into overdrive, searching for a plausible location. "Northern California. He took a job with a traveling construction crew." That was the cover story he'd been telling their parents.

"So you're stuck holding the bag."

Now it was her turn to shrug. "Yeah." Time to bring this back to the treasure because as much as she didn't want his help, she needed it. "I need your help to find the treasure. If we work together, we can split it down the middle. I just need enough to cover Cy's debt."

He shoved his hands in his pockets. "You're still not telling me everything and until you do, I'm not helping."

Snips had been clear about the consequences of telling the truth. As much as she was drawn to Sam, she couldn't risk hurting her parents. "I can't."

"Then it looks like we don't have anything left to talk about."

Judging by his clenched jaw, the smartest move would be to admit a temporary defeat. No matter what it took, she'd make him change his mind about finding Rebecca's Bounty. She reached past him to retrieve her jacket from where she'd laid it on his desk. The movement brought her lips within kissing distance of his mouth. The attraction buzzing between them grew to a deafening level. She paused, hovering near him, her lips parting of their own volition as she stared at his mouth. Images of all the things he could do—all he had done—with his mouth flashed in her mind. Anticipation stretched between them as tangible as an invisible wire. Her clit twitched with need and she squeezed her thighs together.

The slight movement broke the spell. Sam blinked his golden hazel eyes and pulled back.

Sam turned away from her, walked over to the window and stared out at the snow-covered quad. The afternoon sun caught the reddish highlights in his hair. "I spent a summer looking for it, walking every inch of McPherson's Bluff, combing over survey maps and aerial photographs."

"And you think you're infallible, is that it?"

In an instant, a visible sign of pain was gone, replaced with a blank mask. "You don't need to know about me."

"I've read the diary. Rebecca didn't lie. It's out there and I'm going to find it. But I need *you* to do it." She grabbed the notepad on his desk and one of his neatly arranged pens, then scrawled the artist colony's main number. The notepad landed with a thwack on his empty desk. "Call me when you change your mind."

Damn, he looked so forlorn framed by the window and the snowy scene beyond it. She couldn't leave him like this. Just as she knew on a gut level that Rebecca's Bounty was out there, she knew Sam needed her. That made what she had to do even worse. But until they recovered the treasure, maybe she could be that woman he needed right now. She could pretend it was just the two of them with no ulterior motives.

Responding to his unspoken call, she inserted herself between the cold glass and his warm body. The beginning of his five o'clock shadow scratched against her palms as she put her hands on his cheeks and turned his head to face her.

"We're more alike than we're different. I saw the real you in Vegas. You might hide him here, but I know better. You were born for adventure."

Her lips brushed against his, soft and hesitant in spite of her bold declaration. She sucked on his bottom lip and pressed against his lean body, daring him not to respond. Her nipples hardened even with layers of sweaters and leather between them. Fire spread through her and she wrapped her arms around him, pulling him closer.

Sam groaned into her mouth in surrender, his hands sliding down her back to cup her ass and bring her into contact with the hard bulge in his slacks. His lips traced a path along her jawline, ending at her ear, where he kissed the sensitive spot behind her earlobe.

Josie couldn't stop the shiver of pleasure that danced up her spine and she arched her neck to give him better access to the sensitive spots above her collar. When he nipped at the skin, she nearly melted into a puddle of want. Her tits grew heavy and full, testing the strength of her bra's underwire. God, if she didn't pull back now she'd be on her hands and knees before she knew it, and she couldn't do that. One and done, that was her M.O. More than that entailed ties she couldn't have to Sam.

So why had she kissed him in the first place?

She ignored the question and instead pushed away from Sam and all the allure pulling them together.

She rested her forehead against his cheek as his chest rose and fell at the same rapid pace as hers. "Just to be clear, that had nothing to do with anything else. It won't happen again."

She felt more than heard him laugh, the shake of his shoulders underneath her fingertips.

Knowing she had to go now, she stepped back from him and walked away, pausing at the doorway. "Call me when you're ready to go find the treasure."

# Chapter Eight

*S*am squeezed through the crowd on the edge of the Robidoux's Roadhouse dance floor, aiming for the bar and the cold bottle of beer in front of the empty stool next to his younger brother, Chris.

A middle-aged cowboy who hadn't seen his belt buckle in at least a decade thumped his boot on the stage as he sang an upbeat ditty about his ex-wife who had done him wrong. Couples two-stepped in a circle in front of the stage, their boots shuffling against the wooden dance floor, moving in time to the beat.

He passed through a trio of men mesmerized by the action on the dance floor, turned left at the door marked Cowgirls Only and slid onto the barstool Chris had saved for him.

The first swig of cold beer went down smooth and he hoped it would temper the heat eating away at his stomach lining ever since Josie had strutted her sweet little ass out of his office this morning. "Tell me again why you always want to come here, Chris?"

"This is where all the cool multimillionaire lottery winners hang out when they're hiding from pain-in-the-ass accountants."

"Trouble in paradise?"

Chris thunked his bottle down on the polished bar, sending foam spurting out of the opening. "My God, the woman wants to micromanage everything."

"So why don't you fire her?"

His little brother shrugged. "Why let her win?"

"That sounds completely logical."

Chris flipped him the bird and turned his attention back to the packed dance floor. "Ho-lee shit, will you look at that. What is she doing in Dry Creek?" He jammed an elbow in Sam's ribs so hard his beer almost went flying. "It's the waitress from Vegas. What was her name? Jenny? Jessie?"

Immediately, the blood in his veins changed direction and headed south. "Josie."

"Yeah, Josie."

Sam followed Chris' gaze and spotted her on the dance floor wrapped in the arms of an older cowboy. A lightning bolt of want slammed through Sam with so much force he dropped his beer. The glass bottle shattered into a million pieces and people jumped to avoid the mess. Everyone in the vicinity turned to stare and, for once, he couldn't have cared less that he was the center of attention. The dance floor had emptied out somewhat, giving him a clear view of Josie and her partner.

Willie Carson had his right arm snug up against Josie, his palm resting on her hip. He held her left hand in his as they two-stepped. His suspiciously black handlebar mustache kept moving up and down to the beat; no doubt he was telling her when to step. Despite Willie's direction, Josie faltered, thrown off by her partner's double fancy spin. She tossed her head back and laughed, the live band covered the sound, but Sam heard it anyway.

His hands curled into fists. He didn't care if Willie Carson was old enough to be his father. He was going to knock him on his ass if he didn't stop touching her.

"You'd better clean up your mess or they'll kick us out." Chris swiped a rag from the bar and tossed it to Sam.

Brought back to reality, he gathered up the bigger chunks of glass right as one of the bartenders rounded the bar with a plastic bucket and a broom. "Sorry about that."

Sam dumped the glass into the bucket.

"Shit happens, man. I got it." With a few flicks of the bartender's broom, the glass disappeared into the bucket.

An ear-splitting whistle blared. "Josie!" Chris waved at Josie, who had just exited the dance floor.

Her face flushed, she whispered something into Willie's ear, then made her way through the crowd to them. How she managed to move in those tight jeans, Sam had no idea.

His gaze roved higher to the black Western-style shirt unbuttoned to the third button, and his fingers itched to test the strength of that third button, an impulse he stuffed down. Josie was the enemy. No matter what she'd told him in the office earlier, he knew she was holding out on him. Treasure hunters had been after Rebecca's Bounty for years. He wouldn't help—not even if the hunter in this case was more intelligent and sexy than the others.

"Hey there." She stuck out her hand to Chris. "I don't think we've been formally introduced, I'm Josie Winarsky."

"Chris Layton." He made a big show of kissing her knuckles, which made Sam's hackles twitch. "So what are you doing in Dry Creek?"

She nibbled on her full lower lip and dropped her gaze to the floor. "I'm at the Rose O'Neill Dry Creek Artist Colony."

"Very cool, so what kind of artist are you?"

Angry at his own loss of self-control, Sam lashed out. "Con artist."

Josie's head jerked up but before she could respond, Chris—ever the peacemaker—drew her attention back to him. "Ignore him. He's not used to being around such a beautiful woman. I, however, am the fun Layton brother."

His brother flirted like that with every woman he met. Sam never cared before, but this time the move irritated him. Unable to keep his hands to himself, he flicked the back brim of Chris' black cowboy hat. Josie laughed that smooth alto song that made him forget there were other people in the world.

"I figured you two were brothers. So, if you're Mr. Excitement, what does that make him?" She nodded her head toward Sam.

"The closet freak." Chris draped his arm around Josie's shoulder and sent Sam a slick smile. The little bastard knew exactly what he was doing.

"Mmm-hmm, I knew that already. It's always the quiet ones."

Sam's frustration spiked. "I am right here."

"So how long will you be in Dry Creek, Josie?" Chris scooted his barstool back to make more room for her.

"I'm spending the next few months painting."

"Oh, you're doing more than that. You're planning to fit in a little treasure hunting, aren't you? Josie here had Rebecca's diary the night we met in Vegas. Very convenient, wouldn't you say?" His blood pressure pushed into the danger zone at the memory of finding the map in Vegas and crashing down from his post-coital high.

The friendly look disappeared from her gray eyes. "I told you already what happened in Vegas was a coincidence."

"Did you make a copy of the diary before you gave it to me this afternoon? It won't help without someone who knows McPherson's Bluff to guide you, so you might as well go back to Vegas because no one here is going to lift a finger to help."

"What happened between us in Vegas had nothing to do with that treasure." Her bottom lip, the one that had tasted of lime, trembled. "They say what happens in Vegas stays in Vegas, but it seems like you left behind your entire personality."

Heat wound through him. He'd like nothing better than to be Las Vegas Sam, but he couldn't do that in Dry Creek. Here his place was defined. The steady one. The serious one. God, he hated it. And here she was, reminding him of the man he'd become—exactly the kind he swore to Michael he'd never be. His ire escalated and demanded release on the nearest target, blinding him to the unfairness of his actions.

"You were just priming me to get information about Rebecca's Bounty. Somehow you knew I've been searching the historical documents for clues about its location, trying to see what others had overlooked. That's why Vegas happened and why you found me here."

"I didn't know about any of that until you said it. I slept with you in Vegas because I wanted to, not for information but because I liked you and, like a complete moron, I thought you liked me too." She shrugged her shoulders, a tightness visible in her jawline.

Sam searched her face, looking for signs of deception. But instead of glancing away, she held his gaze, righteous indignation blazing in her gray eyes. The unfamiliar sensation of being in the wrong curdled the contents of his stomach. "That was totally uncalled for. I'm sorry."

"Not as much as I am." Josie spun around and threaded her way between bar patrons, her pace slower than before but her head held high.

That had gone completely shitty.

He and Chris sat in silence until Josie's white-blonde hair disappeared in the crowd. When it did, Chris shoved his stool back and stood.

"You are such an asshole."

Yes, he was. "Shut up."

"Yeah, well, I'll see you tomorrow. I'm not sitting here anymore watching you be a dick."

Chris tossed a twenty dollar bill on the bar and stalked away.

Sam stewed in his seat and drank his beer, then another one. He was being a prick. He could admit that to himself. But he had reasons and anyway, it wasn't as if Josie gave two shits about him. She just wanted to use him to find Rebecca's Bounty and dammit, he wanted her anyway. His own lack of control appalled him.

He slammed down the now empty bottle and paid his tab.

Making his way to the door, a laugh stopped him. Her laugh. It pulled him toward the dance floor, near where Josie stood talking to Willie.

"Another dance?" Josie shook her head. "I don't know that your feet could take it."

"Oh, I don't mind. You'll pick the two-step up way before you manage to smash all of my toes." Willie grabbed her hand.

"No." The word was out of Sam's mouth before he even had time to contemplate stopping it. He should keep walking but dammit, he couldn't move from this spot. He couldn't leave knowing someone else touched her. "This dance is taken."

"Oh really?" She crossed her arms. "Willie's the only one who's asked."

Heat flushed Sam's cheeks. "You're going to make me say the words."

"Yep." She leaned back against the hip-high wall surrounding the dance floor.

Willie didn't bother to even try to hide his smirk. Shit. By midnight, half the town would know about this. Heat crept up his spine at the prospect of people knowing his business, of knowing him. The Laytons were known for their wild antics, all except for him. Sam kept to himself and he liked it that way. If he left now, he wouldn't have to worry about being the center of attention.

He moved to leave and caught the disappointment darkening Josie's gray eyes. Regret slugged him in the gut. "Will you please dance with me?"

She cocked her head to one side. "Why should I?"

Something primal awoke within him and demanded he respond to the challenge in her voice. Time for lying to himself had passed. No matter what else Josie desired or how much she was hiding, she still wanted him. And he wanted her. The tension pulling his body tight told of just how much he craved her, no matter her secret motives. Worries of people talking about him faded into oblivion and he stepped closer. The cord of sexual tension between them drew tight, making it hard to concentrate on anything more than the full curve of her bottom lip.

"Because I'm sorry and I want to make up for being a complete asshole. Because even though I know you have ulterior motives, I can't seem to care about your reasons for finding me. I'm just glad you did. And because you want to touch me as much as I want to feel you."

Her long fingers skipped nervously from one button to the next on her shirt, stopping at the deep V opening. "So what is this, a truce?"

"Yes. Let's just forget about Rebecca's Bounty and enjoy a dance."

"One dance? No more accusations or name calling? No more being a jerk?" Her thumb flicked at the top fastened button.

"No." His entire body pulsed in time with his heartbeat, the fate of the world seeming to rest on her next words.

She dropped her hand, straightened her spine and tossed her hair out of her face. "Ask me again."

His cock twitched in anticipation of touching Josie. "Will you dance with me?"

She considered him for a moment, dragging her gaze down his body and back up. "I thought you'd never ask." Josie took his hand and pulled him out onto the dance floor.

He slid his hand across the small of her back, electricity skittering up his arm as he turned her to face him. One hand rested on her hip, the other hand clasped hers. Several inches of air separated their bodies until Josie took a half step forward, eliminating the open space. Her distinct scent of amber and orange wrapped around him, daring him to tighten his grip. He flexed his fingers and slid his hand from her hip to the small of her back, using his still vivid memories of their night in Vegas to trace the infinity tattoo hidden by her cotton shirt.

The drummer kept a steady beat, followed by the slide guitar, and the dancers circled the floor counterclockwise. Closer than Velcro, Josie flowed with him as they took two quick steps and then a slow one repeating the moves as they danced. Really, he should keep an eye out for the other dancers to make sure they didn't run into anyone, but Sam couldn't pull his gaze away from her and the way her cherry-red lips moved as she counted the steps under her breath and watched their feet move in time with the music. Her creamy breasts that he remembered so well jiggled against his chest as she swayed. A burst of pleasure-soaked agony exploded inside him. His gaze wandered down to the soft flesh exposed by her partially unbuttoned shirt. The promise barely contained by that third button elicited a groan of frustrated need.

"Sorry, did I step on your toes?" Josie met his gaze. It took only a second for the worry in her gray eyes to morph into something more carnal.

Attraction tensed his muscles and he whirled her around in a spin as they two-stepped across the floor. When she faced him again, he pulled her close and she rested her head against his shoulder. One platinum-blond curl brushed against his cheek, tempting him to bury his nose in it.

"If you don't kiss me soon," she whispered against his neck. "I'm going to be forced to do something drastic."

"I can't even imagine what fits into your definition of drastic."

"It might involve stripping you down to your tighty-whiteys and having my wicked way with you while the band plays "The Devil Went Down to Georgia".

He let go with a rusty laugh. God, it felt good just to...relax.

"That's the Sam I know." She raised her head and brushed her lips against his. "I don't know why you pretend to be so stiff, but the only thing rigid about you right now is this."

Her fingers grazed his hard-on. The denim of his jeans blocked skin-to-skin contact but the barrier only enhanced the hot factor. "That seems to be the case whenever I'm around you. Opposites attract, I guess."

"Bullshit." She nibbled her way up his neck. "We're so much alike on the inside that it scares the shit out of you."

He stumbled for a moment and nearly ran over another couple. Smiling his apologies, he spun Josie over to the wall. "We need to get out of here."

"Let's go, cowboy."

# Chapter Nine

$\mathcal{J}$osie swept her palm along the wall, searching for the light switch inside Sam's front door. The simple act proved difficult because of the lightning bolts sizzling through her body as Sam's lips ravaged hers. His body pressed her against the open doorframe, his cock nestled against the zipper of her jeans. Buzzing from flash after flash of pleasurable sensation, she circled her hips against his hardness, searching for release.

Seeking to anchor herself to him, Josie threaded her fingers into his light-brown hair, which was as soft and yielding as the rest of him was rock hard and demanding.

"Fuck, Josie, you make me forget who I am," he panted against her neck before kissing his way up, stopping at the sensitive patch of skin behind her ear. He sucked her earlobe between his hungry lips, nipping it lightly.

She stopped breathing. Heat and damp flooded her pussy; an itch building that grinding against Sam couldn't cure. Her need to feel him sliding between her slick folds hit her even harder than it had in Vegas.

Drawing on powers of self-denial she didn't even realize she had, Josie untangled her fingers from Sam's hair and slid one hand up the wall until she encountered the cool plastic light switch. By the time she flipped it on, he was licking the top of her collarbone and sending all kinds of tingling sensations across her skin. Her control flickered like a flame in the breeze. Usually a quick, hard fuck would be enough. Wham. Bam. Thank you man. But not tonight. Not with Sam.

Determined to draw out the anticipation, she pulled out of his embrace and took a few steps backwards. Taking in his living room and its matching beige couch and the identical silver lamps on the innocuous birch side tables, she flicked off her electric-blue heels—so out of place in this den of neutrals. Everywhere she turned were eggshell-colored walls. The only thing interrupting their perfect blandness was a large painting of McPherson's Bluff. Guilt rose as she stared at the reminder of her mission from Snips.

Her conscience struggled to be heard above the roar of lust, warning her to tell Sam the truth. All of it. Damn, she wanted to, but she had no doubt Snips would deliver on his promise to hurt her parents. She and Sam had declared a truce. This was just sex with a hot and willing partner. Nothing more.

"So are you going to offer me something to drink? Show me your etchings?"

"I have plenty to show you but it's not on paper." He moved forward.

She stepped back.

Curious about how far she could push him, she popped open two buttons on her shirt, giving her boobs the breathing room they'd been dying for all night. "But I have an ongoing fantasy of putting you on canvas. Will you pose for me?"

"You know there's little I wouldn't agree to right now." The hunger in his tawny eyes blazed as he stared at her tits.

Men staring at her chest had been a daily fact of life since she'd turned sixteen. Usually she didn't have any response but annoyance. But not with Sam. Having his gaze glued to her boobs sent wave after wave of wanting through her. Pressing her arms together a bit, she pushed her flesh forward so her hard nipples barely stayed contained within her bra's leopard-print silk. Enjoying the mesmerized look on his face, she slipped a finger beneath the smooth material, warm from her overheated skin.

"So adventurous. Just how I like you." Josie traced her finger across the tops of the curves capturing his attention.

"And what can I do for you right now?" He quirked an eyebrow.

Josie crossed the room and sat down on the plain couch, trying to ignore the wetness between her legs in favor of teasing him a bit longer. "Come over here and strip for me. Slow. I have to memorize each line and shadow. It's research, you know."

He didn't move but his gaze flew to her face. "Yeah, not gonna happen."

"Come on, Sam, stop hiding behind that stuffy professor image you've locked yourself into. We both know it's a load of shit. You can be yourself with me."

He hesitated a moment longer, then pushed off the door and strode over to the couch, an intensity in his eyes that had Josie wondering what she'd just gotten herself into. Without saying anything, he slipped a button on his shirt through the buttonhole.

"Is this what you want?" He made quick work of his shirt, spreading it wide and showing off the kind of hard abs no history professor should have. "Should I stop here or go on?"

Mouth dry, she had trouble forming words so she just nodded her head. So much for being in control.

Sam's shirt dropped to the floor and his fingers rested against the button of his jeans but didn't pop it open. Pushed on by a need growing exponentially with every breath, Josie reached out for that button. Fuck the strip tease; she wanted that cock of his inside her.

He pushed her hand aside. "Uh, uh, uh. No touching the talent." A very unprofessor-like grin curled his lips.

Looks like she'd created a monster. "So that's how it's going to be?"

"Yep." He flipped off his shoes and popped open his fly.

The brief glimpse of white cotton vaporized any thought beyond getting to see more.

She gnawed on her bottom lip, mentally begging Sam to hurry it up. Slow? What the fuck had she been thinking when she'd made that request?

He hooked his fingers into his waistband. "Sure you're ready for this?"

Josie gulped and nodded her head. Her pussy ached from unsatisfied wanting and the temptation to drop to her knees, put her mouth level with that white cotton, nearly overwhelmed her.

The moment before her restraint snapped, his jeans slid down his muscular thighs. His hard cock pointed straight at her but remained hidden behind that damn cotton.

"Your turn." His voice barely louder than a harsh whisper screamed out to the desperate need burning Josie's skin, tightening her nipples and making her clit throb.

"For what?"

"I didn't get to look my fill in Vegas, if it's even possible to." He pulled her up from the couch. "Stand here."

Josie stepped onto the oval birch coffee table, but instead of sitting, he stayed close, reaching up to one of the few buttons still holding her shirt closed. His fingers rested there for a moment and he tugged her so she bent forward and his lips were millimeters from the upper curve of her full breasts. His breath whispered against her, but he didn't touch.

Heat swirled through her body—she needed to be fucked now.

No. She needed to be fucked by Sam now. Josie thought she'd explode if he didn't touch her soon,

"God, you smell so good. Do you know how much you've haunted me?" He licked the deep alley between her full breasts. "Now I want more."

"Lucky you." Her attempt at sultry came out a breathy whisper. "You can have all you want tonight."

"Only tonight?"

"Who knows how long this truce will last?" She traced a finger down the two-inch scar tearing a jagged path across his cheekbone.

"I can promise you now, tonight will not be enough for me." His hands spread open her shirt and pushed it down her arms. As it fell to the table, he bent forward, his face traveling south, kissing her stomach and spending time tracing her bellybutton.

Her knees weakened and he tightened his grip on her hips, holding her firm.

The world grew hazy as her endorphins pulled her higher. She'd broken a lot of rules in her life, but always those set by other people. By being with Sam again she was breaking one of her own. One and done. But at the moment she didn't give a damn.

The button of her jeans snapped open and he peeled them off of her, following the path of newly exposed flesh with his exploring mouth. Across her right hip. Down the side of her thigh. He stroked the back of her knee, the tickle barely registering in comparison to the heat building between her legs. She didn't know whether to be happy or pissed off that she was wearing panties. At least the tiny swath of fabric matched her bra. Why that mattered, she didn't know, but she knew Sam would appreciate the coordination. And for some strange reason *that* mattered to her.

As she stepped out of her jeans, Sam worked his way back up her opposite leg, this time kissing and nibbling and licking up the inside of her leg. By the time his mouth was tantalizingly close to her wet pussy, her moans filled the silence of his living room. Josie threaded her fingers through his smooth hair, guiding him toward the juncture of her thighs. When his head failed to move any closer she almost wept in frustration.

"Getting impatient?" His hot breath brushed against her sensitive clit as if she wasn't wearing any panties.

Sam grasped her full hips in his hands and licked the silk material between her legs. At that point, her knees did give out and only his strong fingers around her hips kept her from tumbling off the coffee table. The sound of her panting filled the air as she lost herself in the onslaught of sensation. God, the man undid her and almost made her forget for a heartbeat why she never came back for seconds.

"Enough, Sam." She stepped onto the floor, the Berber carpet rough against her bare feet.

God, he looked delicious standing there in his crisp white underwear. Instead of the muscled bulk of most of her lovers, he had a runner's physique, thin but strong with well-defined abs that didn't require hours in the gym every day. No. He had better things to do than just hone his body, and that turned her on more than a set of six-pack abs ever could. The sexiest thing about Sam was between his ears—not that the hard shaft between his legs was anything to shrug at.

She sucked his bottom lip into her mouth before claiming his lips, sliding her tongue along his. The deliciousness of the moment nearly undid her and she had to pull away.

"What are you thinking?" His shoulders tensed.

"That a girl could get used to fucking you on a regular basis."

He laughed. "Thank God, I thought you'd changed your mind."

"Not about this."

She reached around and unhooked her bra's clasps, letting it drop to the floor. Her breasts, heavy with wanting, tingled with newfound freedom. Her panties hit the floor next. Josie hooked her fingers into his waistband and whipped his underwear down his legs, kneeling in front of him so his cock was at mouth level. She slid the head across her lips, his precum wetting them, before licking from the base to the tip with one lap. Salt, soap and heaven mixed together on the tip of her tongue as she opened her mouth for him.

"Fuck, Josie, you—" Whatever else he'd planned on saying was lost in a moan made of equal parts bliss and torture.

Slow and deliberate, her mouth traveled up and down his shaft setting the pace for what she planned to be a long evening. Nothing else existed right now except for them, and God knew, she'd always appreciate Sam for giving her that. She hoped he'd feel the same after the search for Rebecca's Bounty was over.

Too soon, he stepped back, leaving her hungry to taste more of him.

Josie stood up and sashayed the few steps to where he stood. "Don't tell me you're changing *your* mind now."

He laughed, but there wasn't any humor in the sound. Instead it was more an animal growl that skittered down her spine and made her entire body throb. At that moment, she knew sex with Sam would never be just a fun way to get off. Already her body called out for him like the roulette wheel beckoned the hopeless gambler.

"Come here." He sat down on the ottoman.

Determined not to lose herself completely in Sam, Josie hesitated to regain her mental footing, then grabbed her purse from the floor. She popped the magnetic latch and fished around inside until her fingers contacted the foil square. Prize acquired, she dropped her bag and strutted over to the ottoman.

When Josie moved to sit astride him, he caught her hips. "No, stay right there."

That magic mouth of his went to work on her sweetest spot, his tongue and lips swirling around her clit as two fingers slipped inside her hot slit and rubbed against her G-spot in a rhythm so unhurried, it bordered on cruelty. In and out he worked as she straddled the peak between anticipation and orgasm, unable to fall back or leap forward. Her thighs began to shake as he continued, increasing the pressure inside and outside of her. Needing to steady herself, she tangled her fingers in his hair and begged for release in a tone so desperate she barely recognized it as her own. And that was when he said something, he words muffled so she couldn't understand, but the vibrations of his voice rubbing against her provided that extra push. Everything faded to black all around her a split second before her entire body tensed with a climax that obliterated her bones.

Coming down a moment later, Josie tried to catch her breath. As the blackness dissolved, it was Sam's face she saw first. The tantalizing mouth, slick with evidence of her desire. That little scar on his cheekbone, flushed with color. Those hazel eyes with the golden flecks. His usual shield of coolness was gone, revealing his hungry, adventurous soul.

He ripped the condom wrapper open and unrolled the latex down his thick cock. Watching his hands wrap around himself had Josie squirming as if she hadn't just had a body-melting orgasm.

Her heart hiccupped, but she refused to drop her own defenses enough to wonder why. She'd run far enough out of her comfort zone already tonight. Instead, she lowered her body to his, sheathing his hard cock inside her.

His large hands held her ass, rocking her hips forward, and she lowered herself to meet his thrusts again and again. She arched her back, bending like a bow, pleasure making her quiver. Moving one hand from his knee, she cupped his balls, squeezing lightly, his appreciative moan sending a shiver down her spine.

Just when she thought she'd regained control, Sam slid his hand around and his thumb found her clit, which he pressed in the same quick-quick-slow tempo as the two-step they'd danced at Robidoux Roadhouse. The world exploded around her again and her hips rocketed forward, coming down hard on his cock as the orgasm ripped through her. A few thrusts later and his climax followed.

They sat there for a few minutes with her legs wrapped around his waist and his head resting on her shoulder.

A tightness clamped down on Josie's lungs and a lump threatened to block her throat. Closing her eyes, she locked her jaw and fought to stop the release of emotion.

Damn. Now she wanted more than a single night, but her secrets dangled over her head, ready to drop and shred her happiness at any moment.

"You are amazing." Sam's words tickled her collarbone.

Gulping past the lump, she banished the waterworks with the aid of years or practice. "You're no slouch yourself."

Without disentangling her from around him, Sam stood up and carried Josie to his room. There, they lay down in his king-size bed and snuggled under the tan comforter.

# Chapter Ten

$\mathcal{S}$am's chest hair tickled Josie's nose and she blinked the dryness out of her formerly closed eyes. In the pitch dark of his bedroom, she couldn't see anything, only feel. And that was enough. She sighed and snuggled deeper into the natural pocket where his shoulder met his chest, which just happened to be the perfect size for her head.

His calm, deep breathing made her eyes droop as her lungs moved in time with his. She needed to find her jeans and beat feet out of here, but she ignored the nagging voice of reason. A couple of more minutes to soak this up and then she'd force herself away from Sam's welcoming body, out of his warm bed, and head back to her studio cabin on the edge of town with its scratchy floral comforter and blinking fluorescent bathroom light. Her eyes closed completely and she flung her leg across Sam's thigh. Five more minutes.

A creak sounded across the hall and Josie's eyes fluttered open. A subtle pop echoed in the dark and she woke completely, every sense on alert.

Straining her ears, she picked up on the shuffle of feet against tile.

Snips?

His muscle from Vegas?

Her body tensed and her heart raced. She held her breath for what seemed like an eternity, waiting, dreading what she'd hear next until she couldn't stand the burning in her chest any longer.

Josie unwound her body from Sam's and brought her lips to his ear. "Sam, wake up. I think someone's here."

"Old house," he mumbled and rolled away from her.

"No." She poked him in the kidney. "Someone is here."

He didn't say anything, but he turned onto his back, eyes opened, and stared at the ceiling. A series of muffled thunks and bangs filtered into the bedroom. When she opened her mouth, he silenced her with a shake of his head.

They sat like that as the tree branches scraped against the window, pushed by the gathering wind outside, but no other noises sounded in the dark. Maybe she'd been wrong. It was an old house. A cute bungalow, but still an old house. Hell, it could be her subconscious pushing her to get the fuck out of bed. It was about time she listened to that instead of made-up noises.

Annoyed with herself, she sat up and tossed the comforter off her body. At the same moment her feet hit the floor, a short series of thumps blared in the silence.

Sam bounded out of bed. "Stay here."

"No, Sam, wait. It's Snips." She wrapped her fingers around his forearm, his muscles tensing under her touch.

Another thunk echoed down the hall.

"Stay here."

Before she could blink, he crept out the door and into the hall.

"Yeah, like that is going to happen," she muttered. Lickity fast, she grabbed one of Sam's T-shirts from a chair and pulled it over her head before following him into the dark hallway.

Ignoring the ice-cold tiles, she tiptoed to where Sam stood outside a closed door. Light filtered out through the crack between the door and the floor.

He shot her a dirty look before jabbing a finger in her direction and then pointed it toward the floor.

She gave him a hand signal too, one of the middle-finger, single-digit variety.

A vein throbbed at his temple, but he turned his attention back to the door.

She didn't hear any more noises, but with the blood rushing like white-water rapids through her ears, she didn't take that to mean the invader had left. Nerves strung tight, she flexed her fingers, hoping to ease the adrenaline pounding through her system.

Tension radiated off of Sam as he reached toward the brass doorknob.

His fingers wrapped around it and he slowly rotated to the right.

The light under the door blinked out.

Sam pushed the door open with a whoosh and stormed into the darkened room.

Josie swallowed her scream.

A whump echoed in the room, followed by a thump and a crack. Two shadows grappled, silhouetted against the bay window. One crashed to the floor.

Breaking out of her brain freeze, Josie slapped her hand against the wall until she contacted the switch. Light flooded the room.

A pitiful mewling cry emanated from a man curled into the fetal position on the floor. Latex-glove-covered hands shielded his eyes as he sat up.

"Put your hands down," Sam bellowed from his spot by the window.

"But the light—"

"Put them down!"

The man pulled a pair of night-vision goggles from his face, taking more than a few strands of greasy, shoulder-length gray hair with it. Red suction marks circled his twitching eyes. A ten o'clock shadow darkened a familiar jawline. He caught sight of her in the doorway and broke into a crooked smile that made her heart stutter. Curiosity besting her sense of self-preservation, she stepped closer to him. His eyes didn't have the same gold flecks, but they were the same hazel color as Sam's.

"What in the hell are you doing here, Uncle Harlan?" Sam stood arms akimbo, naked as the day he was born.

Josie's blood started pumping again, but for a whole other reason than fear. She jabbed her short nails into the palms of her hands. This was not the time to get distracted by Sam's tight ass or strong thighs or his...damn, she was a lost cause.

"Does Mom know you're here?"

"No. No one knows I'm at your house."

"Not at my house, here in Dry Creek."

Uncle Harlan cleared his throat. "Um, no. And I'd like to keep it that way. Your mother doesn't like me very well."

"Doesn't like you? You're lucky she didn't fill your skinny behind with buckshot after you stole Rebecca's diary and then lost it in a poker game. The only reason you still get invited to Thanksgiving dinner is because of her promise to Granny Marie. If it was up to mom, she'd bury you hip high in an ant hill."

"That sounds about right." He rearranged himself so he sat with his back straight, the soles of his feet together and interlaced his fingers around his bare feet. All in all, he looked pretty Zen for a guy who'd just gotten caught in the middle of a B and E. "Why don't we meditate on this latest development."

"Are you completely nuts? You just broke into my house." Sam grabbed a small, grimy duffle bag, the contents of which clanged together. "With burglary tools and, what, night-vision goggles?"

Sam's disapproving tone had no impact on Uncle Harlan, who sat straighter. "A concession I had to make to age. I can't lurk around in the dark as I used too, my eyes won't let me. Getting old is hell on the body, but the yoga helps. You should start now, Sam. It does wonders."

"But you had the lights on."

"True, but it's not like I could turn the rest of the lights on in the house."

Sam stomped over to his uncle and loomed over him. "You're after the map, aren't you?"

Uncle Harlan grimaced and waved a hand at the swinging parts of Sam's anatomy only inches from the older man's face. "I don't mind your nudity; however, can you take a few paces back?"

Throwing up his hands in annoyance, Sam roared, "You break into my house in the middle of the night and then complain that I'm naked?"

Peering around Sam's legs, Uncle Harlan wriggled his snowy eyebrows at Josie. "I'm sure you had your reasons. Very good reasons."

"Leave her out of this."

Uncle Harlan grinned his crooked smile and doffed an imaginary hat at Josie. "Sorry to interrupt."

Despite the fact that she should be annoyed at him, she couldn't help but warm up to the bedraggled black sheep of the Layton clan. "Maybe you should go get some pants on; I'll keep an eye on the prisoner."

The old man's eyes twinkled at her jaunty salute to Sam.

Sam rolled his eyes and stomped out of the room, grumbling something about old fools and idiotic treasure hunters.

"So you're after Rebecca's Bounty?"

"For fifty years now."

Fifty years of searching and no treasure? Josie's gut sank as her visions of an easy find faded away. Snips was not the patient sort. He'd send his goon after her—or worse, after her parents—if she didn't find it.

So she'd find it, that's all there was to it.

"Of course, up until this week, I hadn't heard there was a map. Now that changes everything." He nodded and reached out a skinny arm toward her. When she obliged, his bones popped and cracked as she helped him into a standing position. He placed both hands on the small of his back and completed a shallow backbend, setting off a cacophony of pops as his bones set to right.

"I thought yoga was supposed to make you more limber?"

"I'm sure it is, but I don't do yoga. I just said that to bust that young man's chops. He always did get riled quick. I think it's because they treated him with kid gloves after Michael died."

"Who's Michael?"

Uncle Harlan made a *thch-thch-thch* sound and shook his head. "Sad story that is. The boy died so young. Sam never was the same after."

"You need to stop talking right now." Sam stood in the doorway, clad only in jeans, his forehead deceptively smooth considering the venom in his tone.

Uncle Harlan pursed his lips and shook his head. "There's nothing you could have done to save Michael. It's about time you accepted that." His stance softened and the flush drained out of his cheeks as quickly as it had appeared. "Even if you'd found it, the money couldn't have helped him."

A powerful silence descended, pushing down on Josie's shoulders like an unbearable weight. She'd gotten lost in a family drama that had been playing out for years with no resolution.

If Sam noticed the tension, he refused to acknowledge it. He stood as silent and solid as a statue, his face a mask of banality, giving no clue as to his emotions at the moment.

A chastened Uncle Harlan stepped forward, closing the gap between the two men to an arm's length. "Sam, I'm sorry. I didn't mean—"

"If you leave right now, I won't tell anyone you're here."

"Sammy—"

"Just go."

Uncle Harlan sighed and walked toward the door, pausing to rest his hand on Sam's shoulder.

The men stood in the quiet for a few heartbeats, neither speaking nor moving.

The elder Layton gave Sam a quick pat and cleared his throat. "Well then, I'll be seeing you next Thanksgiving."

When Sam didn't say anything, Uncle Harlan flashed Josie an apologetic smile and brushed past her and out the door. The subsequent click of the front door announced he'd left.

Josie looked around at the office's disarray. Papers were scattered everywhere. A stack of books had been knocked to the floor. For most people, this would be a bit more than daily wear and tear, but for Sam's house it equated to disaster-level carnage.

As if unsure about what to do next, Sam trudged to the desk and pushed at the papers on the floor with the tips of his bare toes. "Michael was my twin brother. He died of leukemia when we were twelve."

"Oh God, I'm so sorry."

"I spent an entire summer before he died searching for Rebecca's Bounty, convinced that if I could just find the treasure, we'd have enough money for some magical miracle cure because the treatment he was getting wasn't doing a damn thing anymore." He kept his back to her, misery thickening the natural bass of his voice. "I climbed that stupid bluff every day. Hank, Chris and Claire came with me in the beginning, but by the end of the summer it was just me searching. I must have touched every square inch of limestone, crawled into every crevice and cried on every rock at McPherson's Bluff. Michael died, but I never stopped looking. Ever. If someone was meant to find Rebecca's Bounty, don't you think I would have found it by now?"

Josie took a tentative step toward him, her chest tight. "Sam, what happened with Michael, it wasn't fair but it wasn't your fault."

But Sam wasn't listening to her anymore. Like a man suffering from shell shock, he stared past her, unblinking, confronting whatever demon only he could see. Tension turned his flesh to steel and he clenched his jaw so tightly, Josie worried he'd break something.

Wanting to ease his pain, Josie crossed to him. When he didn't brush off her nearness, she stepped behind him and wrapped her arms around his waist, laying her face against his bare back. They stood intertwined like that for several minutes, until his erratic breathing calmed under her damp cheek. He unwound himself from her embrace and stepped to the other end of the large desk. An all-to-familiar emptiness took the place of his warm body.

"Harlan took it." Sam's shoulders slumped as he gazed into an empty cigar box in the middle of his once pristine desk. "I had hoped, for once, to be wrong."

"The map? It's gone?"

"Only a copy of a fake. I figured if someone came looking, they wouldn't stick around here to confirm its authenticity." All of the anger he'd suppressed burst to the surface in a howl of frustration. "You. Harlan. Who's next to use me because of Rebecca's Bounty? I've been looking for that damn treasure for my entire life. I've wasted years trying to it, to fill some missing part of me. Not anymore."

He flung open a file cabinet and tossed out papers in such quantity the sheaves flew around him in a tornado of fury. Next, he attacked one of the book shelves, chucking worn books to the ground.

Josie slunk back to the doorway as he continued his path of destruction. Who knew better than her the pain of betrayal? God, what had she done?

❧❧❧

Sam paced the length of his home office, running his fingers through his hair and grumbling about false hope and crazy relatives. He'd had enough. No more searching or failed attempts to fix the past. Uncle Harlan was right about one thing. Finding Rebecca's Bounty wouldn't do a damn thing to bring back Michael.

Just as his invectives slowed from a flood to a trickle, something sharp jabbed the arch of his bare foot and pain shot up his leg. He hopped awkwardly on the uninjured foot until he could lean against his desk. Holding his bum foot in one hand, he peered down at the diamond-shaped gold pin piercing his tender flesh.

Michael's Little League pin. Mom had given it to him to wear to the funeral in his twin's memory. Sam slid down the desk and sat surrounded by the papers scattered around the floor and surrendered to the pain.

The cloying scent of lilies, thick in the small church, had nearly choked him. His father sat on Sam's left side, ramrod straight and perfectly still except for the shake in his hands that wouldn't stop. His mother sat on his right side, crying silent tears and squeezing his hand tight as if to keep him from leaving too. A sunburn still chapped his nose and cheeks from his failed attempt to find Rebecca's Bounty and brand-new stitches held together the gash across his cheek, caused by a tumble down one of McPherson's Bluff's steep inclines. Dirt caked under his nails, embedded during fruitless digging after he'd flung the shovel off the bluff in frustration. He hadn't spoken in three days and couldn't imagine ever wanting to again.

He'd denied for so long that his twin was really dying that when it had actually happened, he'd gone into a kind of shock. When he emerged a year later, some part of him had remained trapped in stone— until Josie had shaken it loose.

The woman in question hunkered down beside him, brushed aside the papers and settled next to him. She rested her head on his shoulder and her amber scent tugged him away from his dark memories.

He should shake her off, but her warm flesh pressed against him helped anchor him to the here and now.

"After L.A., I was lost. Usually, I'm the one taking care of everyone, but I couldn't even remember to brush my teeth on a daily basis. Cy came for me, helped me set myself to rights. He's my twin. I can't imagine what it would be like to lose him. I'm so sorry."

The news she had a twin didn't shock him. Intrigued him, maybe, but didn't surprise. That dormant twin part of him must have sensed it and latched on with all its might. Of all the people who knew about Michael, she'd understand most of all.

"The pain, it never goes away. You just get used to it." He relaxed back against the desk. "After Michael died, I was so angry. I didn't speak for a year after he died. And everyone was always staring, whispering when I walked by, calling me 'that poor boy'. They weren't trying to be mean, but I hated being the center of attention, a hook for the town to hang all their pity on. I hated Michael and myself.

"Then, I came across Rebecca's diary. You've read it; you know what her life was like. Her story of giving everything up and starting all over inspired me. I started going out to the bluff again, but it didn't take long until I realized I needed more information. My first words after Michael died were to ask my mother for our family tree. She was taking a tray of baked macaroni and cheese out of the oven at the time and dropped it. The glass pan shattered on the floor, sending shards of glass and pasta flying everywhere. Then she was holding me tight and we were both crying."

He stopped to inhale her scent and brush his cheek against her platinum curls while he regained his iron control over his emotions. God, he'd miss her, but she was an aberration, a wild flower sprouting in the hayfield. Just as the farmer yanked out the trespassing weed, he'd have to remove her from his life. The only true thing he had left was his sense of order and Josie was chaos personified.

Still, he couldn't stop himself from taking one last whiff of her perfume. "I haven't stopped looking for Rebecca's Bounty since that day, but it's time I admit it. There is no treasure."

❧❧❧❧

Josie's stomach tumbled at the hard look in his eyes. He wasn't just talking, he really believed it. The realization struck her as hard as a fist. She'd never be able to save her parents without that treasure.

"I think you need to go." Sam stood and walked to the window, not bothering to turn and look at her. "Go back to Vegas."

Pushing past the prick of his words, she strode to his side, stopping next to him as if to dare him to try to ignore her. "I'm not leaving Dry Creek without the treasure. It's out there and we're going to find it."

His jaw hardened. "Then you're an even bigger fool than that old man. There's nothing for you here."

The words sucker-punched the air right out of Josie's lungs. It took her a minute but eventually she dragged in a ragged breath. "You would think so, but you're wrong."

She swept out of the room, unsure of what hurt more, Sam's dismissal or the fact that leaving him hurt like she was stabbing herself in the eye with a cocktail umbrella. She stuffed her legs into her jeans, slipped on her shoes, swiped her shirt off the floor and considered switching out of Sam's T-shirt before deciding it wasn't worth the bother.

Josie slammed the front door shut behind her and grabbed her keys out of the front pocket of her backpack as she stomped over to her crappy car. She'd figure out a way to get Sam to come around. Her parents' lives depended on it. And dammit, she needed him.

The car door creaked open on rusty hinges. Like her, it was barely holding it together.

# Chapter Eleven

*J*osie scanned the crowd outside of the small house in the middle of nowhere for Sam's auburn-streaked hair. Nearly everyone wore ski caps or these weird hats with earflaps, frustrating her efforts to find him.

The idea had seemed perfect this morning when she'd read about the auction of Beth Martinez's house in the *Dry Creek Gazette*. The article had been accompanied by a photo of Beth and her fiancé, Sheriff Hank Layton. Josie figured Sam would have to show up to his soon-to-be sister-in-law's big event.

She hadn't expected it to be so crowded. There must have been a hundred people milling around in the freezing temperatures. Though her fingers felt like skinny blocks of ice, she'd rolled the dice on finding Sam here and she wasn't ready to give up yet. Perseverance seemed to be her word of the week here in Dry Creek.

Check that. The word of the week had to be desperation. She had to persuade Sam to work with her to find Rebecca's Bounty. Her secret hope was that he'd welcome her into his arms again too, but after she made her confession, there was no way that would be happening. But Sam was a good man. He'd help her save her parents. He had to, time was running out and she didn't expect Snips to offer her an extension.

Josie rubbed her gloved hands together to ward off the arctic-level cold as she hung out at the edge of the crowd at the Martinez auction.

"What in the hell are you doing here?" Sam hissed in her ear.

Heat flooded her body and she was transported to the tropics. "Looking for you, of course."

"Well, you found me. Now go away."

How did he make it through a day without someone clobbering him? "Did anyone ever tell you that you can be a real ass?"

"Happens all the time." His gaze traveled down her body before snapping back up to her face. "Don't you have a real coat?"

"What do you call this?" She held out her leather-covered arms.

"An invitation for frostbite."

Fire seared her skin when his hand landed on the small of her back and he nudged her toward his car.

"Come on, let's warm you up in my car before you freeze to death."

Damn, even his car was tan. This man desperately needed some color in his life. He followed her to the passenger side and opened the door.

"Thanks."

"Even I have manners occasionally."

It looked like a shiny, new show model on the inside. No crumpled candy wrappers or junk mail piled on the passenger seat or even a wet patch of melted snow. She slid into the still warm car and practically melted into the leather seat.

Sam circled around back. A blast of cold air shot into the car when he pulled open the driver's door and sat down. After he shut the door, they sat in silence for a few minutes until he turned the key in the ignition and a hard-driving drum solo blared from every speaker. With reflexes faster than a cat sprayed with water, Sam jammed the radio's off button.

Josie couldn't stop laughing. "It's okay, I'm not going to rat you out for actually being human."

Sam's lips twitched into an almost smile. "No one would believe you anyway."

"Not even your family?"

He snorted. "Especially not my family. I'm as much a black sheep in the Layton family as my uncle Harlan."

"What did he do?"

"He stole Rebecca's diary and lost it in a poker game."

The fact that she ended up with that diary hung unspoken in the air between them.

"And what did you steal to put you in the black sheep category?"

"Nothing. Unlike the rest of my family, I can keep my emotions in check and control my temper. That makes me the blackest of sheep."

Josie laughed so hard her sides ached. "Are you completely out of your mind? Did you forget you lost it and stormed out into the hallway of that Vegas hotel buck-ass naked to accuse me of sleeping with you to get to Rebecca's Bounty?"

The tips of his ears turned scarlet and his jaw went rigid, but Sam didn't say a word. Instead, he put the car in reverse and backed out of the makeshift parking lot, spitting gravel under his tires.

Deciding silence was the better option, Josie fastened her seat belt and watched the scenery fly by. After half an hour of listening to Sam grind his teeth, she was ready to wrest the wheel from him or bail out so he could drive himself off a cliff. If his plan was to piss her off until she would rather sleep with Snips Esposito than work with Sam to find Rebecca's Bounty, he was well on his way to total success. Meanwhile her attempts to glare a hole in his thick skull failed miserably.

"Enough of the silent treatment. Where in the hell are you taking me?"

The car jerked to a stop in front of a closed metal cattle gate secured with a padlock. "Here. Come on, get out and really see it."

Wind whipped at Josie's hair, its cold fingers digging underneath her collar despite her coat being zipped up to her neck.

McPherson's Bluff loomed above them looking like a huge, solid, snow-covered brick. It rose nearly a mile from the flat prairie that reached out in every direction from its base. Off to the left, a gnarled path of sunken ravines snaked out toward the horizon. A wide path had been cut down the center of the monument and a modern road weaved its way up the pine-tree-speckled bluff. Josie couldn't help but admire its fierce, solitary and utterly unwelcoming beauty.

"Wow."

Sam chuckled. "Imagine seeing that from the front seat of a wagon after you've abandoned your old life to create a new one in a place you've never seen and with people you've never met. What kind of person would risk everything to travel through hostile territory for a slim chance at a better life?"

"You sound like you wish you were that kind of person."

"No." He slammed the car door shut and stormed over to her, stopping inches from the tips of her black boots. "I'm not that kind of person. I like order and I like certainty. I like standing in the back of the room away from the attention and the talk. I want steak on Friday nights and pancakes every Sunday morning. I like going to my office at the same time every day and having the same roast beef sandwich for lunch Monday through Friday."

He moved in close enough for her to feel the heat pulsing off of his flushed cheeks. Or maybe it was the heat moving up from her wet pussy that caused the breathless jittering in her stomach. Her entire being focused on him as her nipples hardened in anticipation of the electric flash that would explode inside her the moment they touched.

She should say something, do something but the golden flecks in his hazel eyes held her mesmerized. Josie hung on the edge of a sheer cliff of need—not wanting to pull back, but unable to take that final step forward into the oblivion of passion.

"I have a boring life in a small town where nothing ever happens. My plans for the future involve putting fifteen percent of my salary into my 401K and publishing papers in dry history journals that no one reads. There is no room on my calendar for adventure or treasure hunting with a woman who stands out in the room like a shiny new penny."

His lips were only millimeters from hers, his breath pushing against her parted lips like a heated caress. Josie's body vibrated from toes to eyebrows. If he didn't touch her soon, she would have to pounce on him.

"You probably don't even eat leftovers," he grumbled.

"No."

"Or drive the exact same route to work every day." He drew a gloved finger down the zipper of her leather coat, frustratingly close to her breasts but not touching them.

"Uh-uh." So much of her brain had evaporated she couldn't even form words anymore.

"We're nothing alike." He grabbed her shoulders, squeezing the tender flesh. "I am content with my routine. I don't want to change anything about it. Do you understand me?"

Josie could only blink in response to his growled pronouncement as her heart raced and her body cried out for him.

Sam dropped his hands from her as if she'd burned him and stepped back. "So why do you make me think that I'm missing out on something extraordinary?"

He spun around on one heel and strode to the locked gate, his shoulders slumped. The chain rattled as he shook it in a half-assed attempt to open it. He leaned his forearms against the top railing and looked out at McPherson's Bluff. The rock stood alone in opposition to the rest of the topography, refusing to bow to the winds pushing against it.

"Because maybe deep inside you know you *are* missing something." She moved to his side, wanting to wrap him in her arms but knowing he'd rebel if she attempted to comfort him. "Give yourself permission to take a leap of faith—like those people who traveled across the country. Like Rebecca."

"Leap of faith." He spit out the words as if they were a curse. "I'm trying to save you the heartache of pinning everything on a longshot and coming up a loser, and you want me to take a leap of faith?"

"Yes."

"Look at it. McPherson's bluff is covered in a foot of snow. Half the landmarks on the map are buried. If you have to take a leap of faith, at least be sensible about it and come back in the spring."

The muscles between her shoulder and spine clenched in a stress death grip. "Spring is too late."

"Why, for God's sake?"

"I have to find Rebecca's Bounty or else Snips is going to hurt my parents." Just saying the words out loud for the first time made the whole process seem hopelessly overwhelming.

He turned, a wary interest flickering in his tawny eyes. "Keep talking."

"Cy is working with some sort of hush-hush security group. The Callandriello family is after the governor's daughter and Cy is keeping her safe."

"What in the hell does that have to do with Rebecca's Bounty?"

Snow crunched under her boots as she paced in front of the gate. "Snips works for the Callandriellos and wants to move up the food chain by offering Cy up on a silver platter. He thought the best way to do that was to use me as bait, by telling me Cy owed him forty thousand and that I had to pay up since he couldn't find Cy. He figured I'd freak out, bring in Cy, and bam, he'd have his man. Instead, Cy moved our parents out of Vegas and I hightailed it to Dry Creek. But Snips tracked me and my parents down. I have to produce the treasure—the whole treasure. If I don't, my parents pay the price." Heart kicking against her ribs, Josie came to a stop in front Sam and fought to control the tremble in her voice. "Please, I can't save them without you."

Her panting breath came out in puffs of air, surrounding them like clouds of desperation-tinged hope. She searched his unresponsive face for some sign in his hazel eyes that all wasn't lost, that her faith in him was well placed. That he'd forgive her lies.

The jingle of his phone cut through the tension-filled silence. Without looking away from her, he reached into his pocket and pulled out his cell. "Yeah?"

The neutral mask slid away and anger drew his eyebrows together and sent the vein in his temple pulsing wildly. "I'll be there in twenty minutes." He shoved the phone in his coat and marched to the car. "We have to go. Now."

"What happened?"

"Someone trashed my office and left Uncle Harlan beaten and bleeding on the floor."

# Chapter Twelve

*S*omeone—probably Linc—had done a hell of a job on Sam's office at Cather College, setting off a chaos bomb in what had been the capital of Order Nation. The filing cabinets' empty drawers gaped open like a kindergartener without his front teeth, their contents covering the floor. Books littered the once clean desk, volume upon volume lay where they'd been thrown from the shelf. Worst of all, Uncle Harlan sat slumped in the solitary upright chair, a clump of bloody paper towels pressed to his nose and a wicked shiner turning his right eye an unappealing shade of deep purple as he answered a campus police officer's questions. Uncle Harlan had left Sam's house a bit scraped up, but not bruised and battered like this.

"I'm going to kill that bastard loan shark," Sam growled as they stood in the doorway.

She yanked him out of the opening and down the hall before anyone spotted them. "Don't talk like that. Snips is a shithead, but he's still a guy with muscle and a mean streak as wide as the Rockies. Do not fuck with him. I couldn't live with myself if you were hurt." The truth of the statement hit her like a slap across the cheek, hard and crisp.

Something feral gleamed in his eyes and he kept his jaw clamped shut.

"We have to handle this ourselves or we'll make it worse."

"And what do you recommend we do?" He barely got the question out through his clenched teeth.

"Cards close to the vest. We get Snips what he wants and he leaves us alone."

"Do you really think it will be that easy?"

No, but what other choice did they have than to play Snips' game? "It has to be."

"Another leap of faith, huh?"

Gazing into his lion-like eyes, Josie searched for the man she met in Vegas and had found again last night. The one who would take a chance and step into uncertainty without hesitation. "Please."

"This is idiotic." Sam twisted one of her short curls around his finger. "But I'll do it—my way."

His caveat hung in the air between them, but still relief swept down her spine, lessening the tension holding her lungs tight.

"I was wondering what was keeping you. Now I understand." A man in a brown sheriff's uniform walked toward them, a slight hitch in his gait. He grinned at Josie, his hazel eyes shot with green instead of Sam's gold. "Sheriff Hank Layton, at your service. You are?"

She shook his hand. "Josie Winarsky."

"I'm Sam's brother. Sorry to meet you under these circumstances, but looks like little bro may have ticked off a student. Uncle Harlan said he was waiting for you when someone clocked him a good one. I imagine our mother has a good alibi so who else would have wanted to harm Harlan or go through your stuff?" Hank's mouth smiled, but his eyes stayed cop serious. "Why don't you update me on what's going on in your life."

စာစာစာ

Sam hadn't been fooled by Hank's aw-shucks smile since he'd been six years old and his older brother had conned him out of the last Rolo in the pack. Hank's question was anything but innocent, but this wasn't Hank's fight. Hell, he didn't even have jurisdiction on campus. Whatever had happened in his office had to do with the folded map hidden away in Sam's inside jacket pocket, and he'd be damned before he brought his brother in on another improbable hunt for Rebecca's Bounty.

But that was the kick of it. The more time he spent with Josie, the more the impossible started to seem feasible.

"What's going on in my life? Not much." Unless, of course, you counted the bombshell next to him, the break-ins or finding a long-lost treasure map.

"Uh-huh." Brother translation: Bullshit.

"Is Uncle Harlan okay?"

"His nose is busted up pretty good, but he'll live." Hank shrugged his shoulders. "So I was about to call Mom before she heard the news through the town gossip mill, but figured I'd talk to you first to find out what's really happening."

As threats went, this was a good one. Glenda Layton had been a helicopter parent before there was even a word for it. Since she'd retired, she'd devoted most of her energy to trying to run her four children's lives, something the siblings resisted more than a cat fights taking a bath.

A crash in the office sounded before Sam got a chance to respond to Hank's challenge. He, Hank and Josie sprinted toward the ruckus.

"I'm telling you, I didn't do this!" Uncle Harlan shook with emotion as he jabbed his finger into the campus police officer's chest. "I was sitting her waiting for my nephew when I heard a noise. The next thing I know, I'm waking up in here staring at the spit-shine of your boots."

The man, identified as Smith on his name badge, swept aside Uncle Harlan's finger. "The office was unlocked when you entered?"

A flush rose fast across Uncle Harlan's cheeks. "Not exactly."

"And exactly how was it?" The officer waited, eyebrows arched, for whatever tale Uncle Harlan planned to spin.

Sam couldn't wait to hear this answer himself. He locked his office whenever he left—and sometimes when he was still there, depending on the grades he'd given out during midterms.

"Alright, I may have fiddled with the lock a bit, but I did not do this." Uncle Harlan waved his hand toward the worst of the disaster zone.

"Uh-huh." Smith glanced up at Sam. "Any ideas?"

*Plenty.* "Not a single one."

Smith eyeballed him skeptically, but Sam refused to give an inch. His orderly world had been shuffled and he would be the one to set it to rights again.

"Can I go now? I need to go get my nose X-rayed."

Smith leveled a cop-to-cop gaze at Hank. "Can you vouch your uncle won't disappear?"

"He won't unless he wants to miss out on Mom's baked mac and cheese for the rest of his life." Hank led Uncle Harlan to the door, stopping just under the archway. "We'll talk soon, Sam."

Not if he could help it.

After a quick discussion with Smith, Josie and Sam were back in his spanking-clean Volvo, a stark reminder of the mess they'd just left. Damn, the whole thing pissed him off and put him right in the center of attention for Dry Creek's gossips. The place he'd hated being more than anywhere else.

Then again, he seemed to be doing all sorts of things that were out of character whenever he was near Josie. It wasn't that she pushed him to be someone different. Strangely enough, he just felt more himself around her.

Josie cleared her throat. "So where to now?"

"O'Neill's." The single word was all he could manage as he pulled out of the parking lot, the smell of her amber perfume swirling around him in the enclosed space, distracting him from the plan he'd started working on as soon as he'd gotten the news about the break-in. Years of research about Rebecca and the family jewels she'd supposedly brought West, along with the map in his pocket, meant he had the best chance of finding Rebecca's Bounty. Once he found it, the woman who beguiled him could go back to Vegas and his life would return to normal. Exactly what he wanted. He didn't give a damn about the treasure itself. Now he wanted to find it just to check that off his to-do list and get his life back to the way it always had been. And should be.

They drove in silence, if not in peace. Josie sat ramrod straight in the passenger's seat, the afternoon sun glinting in her hair as they drove south from Dry Creek. Tension as tightly wound as the platinum curls surrounding her heart-shaped face filled the car's interior.

"Okay, so what's the plan you're cooking up in that head of yours?" She arched an eyebrow at him.

"What makes you think I have a plan?"

"Of course you do. You wouldn't make breakfast without a plan so you sure as hell wouldn't go on a treasure hunt without one."

"You know me that well, do you?"

"You're the one who just told me all about how much you love routine, but I know plenty more about you than just that. I know you love your family and this town. I know you are curious about everything. And I know that if you'd ever let anyone close enough to scratch your anal-retentive surface, they'd find there's so much more to you than tan furniture and mad organizational skills."

Sam concentrated on the empty road ahead of them much more than needed. He had no clue how to respond to her declaration. On unsure emotional ground, he resorted to the best self-defense move he had—being a prick.

"What makes you think I'm going to help you find the treasure? Maybe I'm planning to turn you and that buffoon Linc over to Hank as soon as I get back to town."

For once, Josie didn't have a smart-mouthed rejoinder—something Sam didn't realize he'd miss until it wasn't there.

The fallow, snow-covered fields whipped by as they sped down the highway, clocking in at fifteen miles over the speed limit. Being the sheriff's brother in a small town had its benefits, but getting out of speeding tickets from the state patrol wasn't one of them. He eased his foot off the gas and settled back into a more professorial pace. Much more like him.

"Are you going to tell Hank?"

Her soft question thrummed his conscience. "No, I won't tell him."

"So you'll help me find Rebecca's Bounty?"

"No." He was going to find the treasure on his own. At this point, getting her any deeper involved than she'd already made herself would just put her in more danger, and he wasn't willing to risk that— even if they did have to go their separate ways. Josie had burrowed her way into him, making a place for herself in the nooks and crannies of his soul that had stayed vacant for far too long. If he wasn't careful, he'd never be able to get her back out. Hell, it was probably too late.

"Then what is your plan?" Her cheeks had turned beet red.

He parked the car in front of the only guest cabin at O'Neill's where the windows hadn't been shuttered for the winter. "Not to see you until I have the treasure."

# Chapter Thirteen

𝑈nder the cover of darkness, Josie inched up the window to Sam's house. Her held breath burned in her chest as she strained to hear the slightest noise—or the blaring of an alarm system. After two break-ins in two days, if anyone in this small town needed a security system, it was him. But instead of an alarm, the only sound she heard was the rushing of blood in her ears.

Light bounced off the glass and Josie ducked behind a snow-covered bush. The beam hadn't come from inside, but from a car rolling toward the house. As it neared, Josie picked out the Dry Creek County Sheriff's decal on the passenger door. The cruiser drove slowly down the block and past Sam's pin-neat yard. Even though she knew the evergreen shrub shielded her from exposure, the urge to skulk away didn't abate until the cruiser turned the corner.

She didn't know where Sam had hidden the map, but she hoped like hell it was filed away in his office just waiting to be liberated.

After he dropped his bomb earlier in the car before dumping her at the cabin, she'd gone shopping. She now owned a heavy coat, gloves and some butt-ugly hiking boots that could withstand the snow while she hunted down Rebecca's Bounty. Glancing down, she saw the ankle-deep snow surrounding her new boots but her toes were toasty warm inside. Grudgingly, she had to admit the boots felt much better than the shoes she'd brought with her from Vegas.

*Enough procrastinating, Winarsky. Just climb in the window already.*

Girding herself for her first breaking and entering, she pushed the window the rest of the way up, then grasped the shoulder-high ledge. It took a couple of tries, but she managed to haul her ass through the window, balance precariously for a few seconds with the ledge biting into her hips and then she oh-so-graciously slid face first onto the floor. She remained immobile for a few minutes, her right cheek on the cool hardwood floor, listening to see if her entry had been detected. Getting to catch her breath was icing on the cake.

After examining the world's smallest dust bunny under Sam's desk for a few minutes, Josie figured her career as a cat burglar had begun in earnest. Time to get off the floor.

She targeted the file cabinet first, stepping as softly as possible while wearing heavy hiking boots. Every whispered clomp on the wood floor made her blood pressure shoot higher.

Finally at her destination, she pulled the metal handle on the drawer marked Q—S. Flicking her fingers across the files, she discovered the fat file marked Rebecca's Bounty. She'd say one thing for Sam's intense organizational skills: he sure made B and E easy. Josie plucked the file from its spot and shuffled through the papers inside in search of the map or another clue that would help find the treasure. True, she didn't know exactly what she was looking for, but it had to be there.

"Nice boots."

Josie jumped at the sound of the all-too-familiar voice that had called out her name the other night as he'd squeezed her ass and pounded his cock deep inside her.

The overhead light snapped on. Sam sat in a chair by the office door, wearing only a pair of navy pinstriped pajama pants and a crooked smile. "Looking for this?"

"Yes." The man or the piece of paper rolled up in his hands? Fuck if she knew.

Deliciously tousled, he didn't look anything like an uptight history professor. Gone were the starched collars, replaced with rippled abs and an ornery glint in his tawny eyes. Josie had to avert her gaze before she drowned in a testosterone wave. How many times had she challenged him to stop hiding behind the ironed Chinos? What the hell had she been thinking? A shiver ran up her spine.

"And you were just going to take it and then hunt down Rebecca's Bounty on your own, huh?"

"Yes." The short answer was all she could manage without drooling on herself as the memory of trailing her fingers through the springy hair dusting his pecs hardened her nipples. Her gaze followed his happy trail to where it disappeared beneath his string-tie waistband, the growing bulge a bit lower giving away that he wasn't unaffected, either. The realization sparked the synapses in her brain, pulling her out of the haze of lust.

Leaning forward until his elbows rested on his knees, Sam flashed a predatory smile her way. "That's not going to happen."

Irked at his overblown confidence, Josie cocked out a hip and curled her lips into a sardonic smile. "Says who?"

"Reality." He waved the sheet of paper at her. "Without this, you don't know where the starting point is. You're not familiar with the area. And I think I'm putting it mildly when I say you're not exactly the outdoorsy type."

Right, right and right. She hated that. "I figured Uncle Harlan would probably be willing to help me look."

Sam grinned. "If he was still in town, I'm sure he'd be more than happy to help. But one visit from Mom while he was in the ER and he hoofed it back to his home in Oklahoma."

The urge to scream her frustration nearly overwhelmed her. Every nerve in her body pinched and pulled and heat washed over her skin like a tsunami of anger. Her life had gone completely out of her command. For all the shit she gave Sam about being an anal-retentive control freak, she was his Xerox copy in every way except color. Not something she wanted to clue him in on—ever.

"So that leaves you."

"Yep." His eyes crinkled at the corners in a way that made her stomach do a flip.

Damn her traitorous body and that supreme look of confidence on his handsome face. He thought he'd won, the little shit. Time to regain the upper hand, though how the hell she lost it still baffled her. "You're not getting rid of me. I'm going with you in the morning."

"Well, looks like we'll be partnering up after all." He leaned back in the chair, not even trying to conceal the look of superiority on his face. "Working with me will be a lot easier than clocking me over the head with a blunt object and trying to figure out the starting point on your own."

She hefted up a thick book about the history of Dry Creek County. Just holding it in her hand made her wrist shake. "I don't know, you bring out the compulsion to chuck things in your direction."

His deep laugh caressed her skin as he bolted up from the chair. In an instant, he stood beside her. Her skin vibrated at his nearness and yearning filled her like a fast-building summer storm.

One of his long fingers traced down the open V of her black T-shirt, stopping only when he reached the pointed end. There he lingered, not pulling her shirt lower but also not removing the digit. Her pulse raced.

"We already know we work well together in private." His lips teased along her temple. "Why not see how we function in public?"

"Why the change of heart? I thought you were going all Lone Ranger on me?"

"Because tonight just proves you'll dog my steps no matter where I go." He pulled a curl straight and let it boing back into place.

"True." Being within three feet of Sam Layton for longer than five minutes had her squeezing her thighs together in a vain attempt to ease the ache building in her clit. But she couldn't see a way around it. If she wanted to save her parents, she needed the map and a guide. She needed Sam. "So let's do this."

"Since you asked so nicely." He unrolled the paper and laid it down in the middle of his desk, securing the edges with a magnifying glass on one end and a cornhusk paperweight on the other.

Josie couldn't hold back her groan. It wasn't the treasure map, but instead another damn map.

"This is a historical map of Dry Creek County." He pointed to a rectangle in the northwest corner, his thigh pressing from knee to hip against hers. "That is McPherson's Bluff. The marking behind it represent the badlands."

"What are badlands?" Her voice cracked on badlands as she tried to ignore the sexual havoc his nearness evoked.

"It's a barren area that's suffered serious erosion. It has lots of dry ravines and rock formations. Even back in Rebecca's day, it was an inhospitable place to be." His finger traced a line a few inches east. "This was Rebecca's homestead, the place she bought after leaving the wagon train. People have been using this as the starting point for a treasure hunt for decades and coming up empty."

"So we won't go there."

He shook his head. "Not necessarily. It makes the most sense since that's where Rebecca spent most of her pre-married life in Dry Creek. The others didn't have the map, so we can't discount the homestead right away."

"Wait, you said *most* of her pre-married life."

"That's right. Turn to page forty-eight in the book you were going to toss at me."

Josie flipped open the tome, flicking the pages until she got to the right one. "Mrs. Joseph McNerny."

"Bridgette McNerny was a widowed mother of six who had a farm here." His finger slid a few centimeters southeast. "This is where Rebecca stayed right after giving up on going further west on the Oregon Trail. She was there for only a month."

"Has anyone searching starting there?"

"A few, but again, they didn't have the map so they were just marching toward McPherson's Bluff, digging at any spot that looked promising."

"And to think the map was hidden in the diary the whole time."

Sam pushed away from the desk, his hazel eyes focusing on her with as much intensity as if he touched her. "We miss all kinds of treasures that are right in front of us."

The invisible line of attraction pulling them toward each other strengthened. God, he undid her. If she didn't watch it, she'd lose focus, and with her parents' safety on the line, that couldn't happen. *Forget the lust and get back to business.*

Forcing her attention away from his defined chest, she turned her back to him and stared at the map. "So how do you want to work this?"

"We head out at first light, which is in a couple of hours, so you might as well rest here."

Now that sounded dangerous. "I don't think that's a good idea."

He drew a line of fire across the small of her back. "Why's that?"

"We need to stay focused."

Sam glanced out the darkened window. Not even a tweet filtered in through the opening. "Dawn isn't for a few more hours."

"Just enough time to form a decent plan. Come on, you're Mr. OCD, don't tell me you're willing to just fly by the seat of your pants."

A heavy quiet filled the room. Sam strolled over to the filing cabinet and slid shut the drawer she'd left open. He flicked away an imaginary piece of dust from the metal surface. "Maybe I'm obsessed by something other than order these days and am willing to shake things up a bit."

That woke up the butterflies in her stomach. The truth of it was she didn't want to leave. Hadn't wanted to since that first night in Vegas. If it had been anyone other than Sam, would she have spent so much time trying to get him to partner up in the hunt for Rebecca's Bounty? No. She would have taken what she needed and pushed forward blindly into the unknown. All by herself.

But being on her own had never felt lonely—not until she'd met Sam.

She glanced down at the tattoo on the inside of her wrist. *Adventure is worthwhile in itself.* How long had it been since she'd lived up to that motto? Not since L.A. For too long she'd let cynical bravado take the place of an open mind and free spirit. The one-night stands had been fun, but she'd never spent a second night out of fear of misplacing her trust again. Nothing had been stopping her from seriously painting in Vegas except for her own doubts and insecurities. So she'd dabbled and played instead of creating something that stirred her soul.

What a liar she'd become. Worst of all, she'd been lying to herself.

All this time, Josie had been pretending to be this brassy, ballsy chick when in reality she'd been hiding in plain sight, becoming just as emotionally closed off and controlling as the man in front of her. If he could break loose a little, so could she.

"Forget it. Just be back here in two hours." He'd pulled back from her, his flirting demeanor replaced by a tension that stiffened his muscles and put a bit of a snarl to his mouth.

Suddenly jittery, Josie swallowed past her nerves. "If it's okay, I'd like to stay."

# Chapter Fourteen

$\mathcal{S}$am flipped the switch above the kitchen sink and the small florescent bulb blinked twice and then buzzed to life. Obsessed with her. Whatever possessed him to say that? Intrigued, a bit confused maybe, but he wasn't obsessed. Old man Freud laughed at him from the grave.

"Here, let me get the mugs." Josie's shoulder brushed his as she opened a cabinet.

Caught off guard by her nearness, he fumbled the bag of coffee. It hit the floor with a thump and dark beans rolled across the beige tiles. They crouched down to grab the beans. Sam's head cracked against Josie's, knocking them both back.

He rubbed his cheekbone, now intimately aware of what he'd be in for if he ever switched places with a gong. *Impressive, Layton. Way to wow her with your amazing skills.*

"Are you okay?"

She snorted and massaged the top of her head. "I'll live. Man, and I thought I had a hard head."

"You do." Sitting back on his heels to put some distance between them, he fought the urge to push her hands aside so he could check her for injury. *Oh fuck it.* "Here, let me look."

His fingers slid through her smooth curls. Right away he realized she wasn't hurt, but he kept parting her hair and pretending to examine her head while he inhaled her amber perfume. The woman sent his blood flowing south and turned him into a bumbling idiot without even trying. The smart move would be to stay the hell away from her, but his brain had lost the fight the moment she'd walked into his lecture hall.

"What do you think would have happened if we'd met here in Dry Creek instead of Vegas? If no one had ever found that map?"

Sam's gaze locked on the tile beneath his knees. Bland. Colorless. Beige. That's what his life would be like without Josie. He'd flirted his way out of his comfort zone in Vegas, drawn in at first by her bombshell looks but held tight by the intelligence and courage behind the pretty face. He never would have had the balls to even approach her in Dry Creek.

"I don't know."

Her gray eyes didn't betray any reaction to his words. "Well, we'll never know anyway. I'll live, so let's get that coffee made." She brushed his hand from her head and stood up, cupping a handful of coffee beans in her palm.

"Josie…" Sam rose to his feet, bringing his body in line with hers from toes to lips.

He had so much to say to her, to explain that in Dry Creek he'd been playing the same role for so long it was nearly impossible to change. Meeting her in Vegas had been like getting struck by lightning, a one in a million chance to find a part of himself that he thought had died along with Michael. The part willing to take a risk, that wasn't afraid to stand out in the crowd.

But despite his PhD and Scrabble-worthy vocabulary, his mouth couldn't form the words.

Instead, he lowered his lips to hers, trying to tell her everything he couldn't utter out loud. His hands found her hips and he drew her closer, eliminating any space between them until her T-shirt-covered breasts caressed his bare chest.

The coffee beans spilled from her hand, pinging across the tile floor, and she wound her arms around his neck, fingers tangling in his hair. She moaned against him and Sam took full advantage, slipping his tongue between her lips to curl around hers.

He couldn't feel enough of her, taste enough of her, have enough of her. God, would he ever be able to?

He smoothed his hands down her hips, the denim of her jeans barring him from feeling the soft flesh of her curves. The thick material frustrated him while at the same time the can't-touch-me factor heightened his need. Curling his fingers around her inner thighs, he spread her legs as he lifted her higher until her long limbs wrapped around his waist. Her hot pussy pressed against the hard cock still shrouded by the thin cotton of his pajama bottoms.

Needing to taste more of her, Sam broke the kiss and trailed his lips across her jaw, stopping only once he reached her earlobe, eliciting another moan.

She arched her neck to provide him with better access and undulated against his dick, precum already moistening the tip. The things this woman did to him. Not just with her body, but she seemed to know him almost better than he knew himself. He loved seeing the challenge in her gray eyes whenever she called him on his bullshit. Josie pushed him, made him want to be more, be better.

Her short fingernails scraped against his chest, bringing him back to the matter at hand: showing her what he couldn't put into words. She flicked his flat nipple, circling it with her thumb. Impatience vibrated off her heated skin. Wanting to stoke the flames, he abandoned her earlobe for the creamy flesh of her long neck, nibbling his way down the long column as he lowered her feet back to the ground.

Electricity sparked across his skin when her pink tongue lapped at his nipple, the normally sedate nub coming to life under her wicked mouth. He grasped the soft material at the bottom of her thin T-shirt, holding on to it as she slithered down to her knees until his hands were left holding an empty black shirt. Her mouth closed over his prick where it tented the material of his pajama pants and the world lost focus. He arched against her even as his brain tried to resist her siren's lure.

It took every last bit of sanity still in his grasp to step back and recall his purpose.

Staring up at him with her big gray eyes that had darkened to steel, Josie licked her lips. Her hard nipples fought against the sheer red of her bra. Unable to stop himself, he reached inside one cup and freed one a full breast. The porcelain of her skin contrasted starkly with the scarlet lace. Without prompting, she rolled one pink nipple between her thumb and finger while her free hand squeezed her still-covered tit. Fuck, she looked delicious.

His hands itched to reach inside his pants and stroke himself until he came all over her milky skin. His cock bobbed with excitement at the idea. Instead, he reached out and captured her chin, his thumb raking across her bottom lip and dipping inside. Never losing eye contact, she sucked and curled her tongue around the thick digit.

"You want my cock in that sweet mouth of yours, Josie?"

She nodded and increased the power of her suction.

"Good. But I need to taste you first, every inch of you."

He reached down and picked her up and strode over to the table, where he laid her down. With hands shaking from the intensity of his wanting, he made quick work of the button on her pants, peeling them off her, revealing her long legs. He lifted her left leg into the air, putting her ankle at his mouth's level. A perfect place to begin. His lips traveled the miles from her ankle to the apex of her thighs, reveling in the smooth skin and strong muscle that twitched under his attentions. When his tongue slid along her wet nether lips, she arched her back and called out his name.

Tension tightened her body underneath him and he circled her opening with his thumb before plunging it in and out in slow repetition. He sucked on her clit in an unrelenting rhythm and relished her mews of pleasure that grew in their voracity when he added his tongue back into play. She grabbed his head, pushing him deeper. He complied and her body went rigid underneath him with orgasm.

Sam raised his head and took in the wanton sight of her, tousled and clad only in her bra as her chest heaved. Something unlocked in him as he stared down at the princess and the dragon tattoo on her arm. So hard and so soft at the same time.

Ferocious. Brave. Smart. Beautiful. Everything he ever needed.

"I think you've ruined me for the night." She smirked and sat up. "If not longer."

But the intensity of the kiss she delivered belied her words. Their hands and mouths were everywhere at once, stroking heated flesh and pushing the desire to higher peaks. Somehow in the process, her bra disappeared and his pajama pants melted away. Naked and hungry, they stared at each other, the challenge and need in her eyes unmistakable.

"Condom?" She arched an eyebrow. "No worries, I'm on the Pill."

"Josie ..." Again, words failed him when confronted with the force of nature that was Josie Winarsky.

She glanced down for a second before raising her eyes and staring into his soul. "Let's not talk, Sam. Not now."

Her fingers curled around his stiff cock and she stroked, her thumb sweeping over the head and spreading the moisture on the tip and he forgot he could even speak. His body did the talking for him and he grasped her legs again, bringing her ankles to his shoulders. He clutched her hips in his hands and in one bold push, buried himself to the hilt in her wet pussy. Her honeyed walls squeezed him and withdrawing, even a few inches, bordered on torture. Josie dug her heels into his shoulders and used it to leverage herself as she undulated against him. Pleasure began to build at the base of his spine.

Josie widened her legs and slid them down his side until she wrapped them around his waist. Seizing the opportunity to bring her closer, Sam reached down and brought her up from the table. Face-to-face, she gripped his shoulders, her nails digging crescents into his skin. Her ass jiggled in his hands as she rode him hard.

He lowered himself to a chair and spun her around so she faced away from him. He watched the play of her muscles and the deep green of the vine tattoos across her back as she took him deep, wrapping him inside her warmth. Needing to touch more of her, he reached around her and slid his finger into her slick folds, then circled her clit. She collapsed back, resting her head on his chest, and little whimpers that sounded halfway between heaven and hell escaped her lips.

Sam matched the increasing speed of her hips with his fingers on her clit. As her body turned rigid, he grasped her nipple between his thumb and forefinger, pulling it taut. She screamed her climax around them, her pussy clenching his cock, putting him in exquisite agony.

Once her breathing settled a bit, he pushed her forward off his cock, nearly desperate to come now. He led her back to the table, where he bent her forward until her plentiful tits rested against its wood top. He settled between her spread legs, parted her ass cheeks with his hands and pushed forward into her welcoming pussy.

He wanted to take it slow, but she felt so fucking good. Holding onto her waist, he brought her back onto his cock with forceful strokes, sliding into her as if he could find the secrets to the universe in her depths. The heady scent of sex filled the air around them and the sound of skin slapping against skin and heavy breathing echoed throughout the kitchen.

The tingle in his spine spiraled out to his limbs and his balls tightened. His release immobilized him and his entire body went stiff.

It took a minute for his vision to return. The sight that greeted him was Josie looking coyly over her tattooed shoulder, her curly platinum hair tossed helter-skelter around her head. Withdrawing from her was almost beyond him, but her position couldn't be comfortable.

As soon as he left her, everything felt...off.

Josie scooped up her clothes. "I'll be right back."

She disappeared down the hall and Sam yanked on his pajama pants. The first rays of dawn turned the indigo sky a thousand shades of pink and orange. A new day. A second chance.

The shuffling behind him announced Josie's return.

"So how do you like your eggs?"

A deep voice chuckled. "Scrambled, lots of salt. How 'bout you, Linc, you want some eggs?"

The man's voice sent Sam into attack mode, but oblivion came crashing down before he could form a fist.

# Chapter Fifteen

$\mathscr{J}$osie splashed ice cold water on her face in a vain attempt to harden the mush her brain had become. Her heart she could understand, but her mind wasn't supposed to fall prey to Sam's deft fingers or that flicker of something more than lust that had flashed in his tawny eyes. Of all people, she should know better than to believe, but she did.

She thunked down onto the toilet lid and cradled her head in her hands, her stomach weaving as if she'd stepped off the mother of all roller coasters.

A whack sounded in the kitchen, followed by a groan and a thump that made the floor reverberate under her.

She sprinted down the hall and her heart screeched to a halt in the kitchen doorway.

Snips, shadowed by Linc, loomed over Sam's crumpled form. "Miss me?"

The snide remark yanked her back to reality. Her jaw snapped shut, adrenaline spiked and she shot herself at the power-hungry shithead who had turned her life upside down.

Her right fist slammed into his eye socket, sending him stumbling back. She grabbed his head between her hands and banged it down as she brought up her knee.

Meaty fingers wrapped around her arms, yanking her away from the subject of her wrath. She kicked her feet back and tried to wiggle free, but Linc's grip couldn't be broken. Josie let loose with a primal yell.

"Shut the fuck up, bitch." Snips snarled at her, his left eye already puffing up.

Linc freed one of his hands to slap over her mouth.

Snips dropped a duffle bag to the ground and dug out a roll of duct tape. Grunting, he dragged Sam's unresponsive body to a kitchen chair and made quick work of taping his arms and legs to it. For good measure, he wrapped tape around Sam's chest, tying him to the back of the chair.

"This motherfucker isn't going anywhere." He pulled a switchblade from his back pocket, hitting a button to expose the thin but deadly blade.

Panic flooded Josie's system. She thrashed in Linc's iron grip and tried to bite the palm that was still cemented over her mouth. Immobilized, she could only watch and pray for the best possible outcome. Survival for them both.

Snips ignored her failed attempts to gain her freedom. He sliced off a five-inch strip of duct tape and slapped it across Sam's mouth. Then he bitch-slapped Sam with the back of his hand. One. Two. Three times.

"Wakey, wakey, Professor Punk Ass."

Finally, Sam blinked, confusion clear in his eyes, but the moment he spotted Josie locked in Linc's arms, his gaze cleared. He strained to reach her, but his bonds held tight.

"I warned you what would happen if we ever met up again." Snips slid the wicked blade down Sam's cheek, drawing a thin line of blood. "Now it's time to pay the piper for interfering with my plans."

With vicious efficiency, he dug the blade into Sam's cheek, tracing the line of his scar but lengthening it by at least two inches. Blood streamed from his cheek and down his neck.

"Don't worry, head wounds bleed like a bitch, but you won't die. You'll just have a nice reminder of what happens when you mess with James Esposito." Snips wiped the bloody knife blade across Sam's bare chest, opening thin slices across his pecs, then clicked it shut. "Remember that when you finally get loose. Follow us and the penalty for you and the girl will be much steeper."

The loan shark strutted to the door. "Come on, we need to get out of here before the neighbors see us stuffing this piece of ass in the trunk."

Josie screamed against the palm blocking her mouth and struggled to twist herself enough to maintain eye contact with Sam as Linc hauled her out the door. Instead of the fear or anger she expected to see in his hazel gold eyes, she only saw confidence. Didn't he realize how close he'd come to death? Didn't he know how lucky he was?

He didn't blink, didn't look away but instead held her gaze. Just as Linc crossed through the doorway, Sam nodded his head as if to tell her it would all be okay.

Snips rewarded him with a vicious jab that knocked Sam's head back with a snap.

Linc tossed her over his shoulder and she knew everything was far from alright. They were down the hall and out the front door in a matter of moments. True to his threat, Snips hit a button on the car's key fob and the trunk popped open. Linc dumped her in and slammed the lid shut, leaving her in darkness.

Josie fought against the panic bubbling up in her chest and threatening to squeeze her lungs closed. Her knees pressed against her breasts as she lay curled in the fetal position with her right shoulder touching the sealed opening.

"At least you're not claustrophobic," she mumbled to herself.

The car's motor roared to life and the smell of gas permeated the space. Inertia tried to move her body when they turned a corner, but the close confines of the sedan's trunk negated any motion but the bare minimum. After a few minutes they picked up speed. The highway? Was he taking her back to Vegas? She didn't even want to think about what Snips would do to her there.

ৎৡৎৡৎৡ

Blood spilled down Sam's face from the gash across his cheekbone. When the stream hit his chin, it met up with the line of red liquid gushing from his nose. With his body immobilized by the gray duct tape, he could only stare at the cordless phone no more than three feet away. The anger burning in his gut would have to wait for release. First, he had to get Josie.

He strained against the sticky bonds holding his wrists tight against the chair arms, his ankles to the chair legs and his chest to the upright wooden back. The tape yanked out several arm and chest hairs but failed to tear.

The image of Josie tossed over that thug's shoulder like a fifty-pound bag of dog food flashed in his mind. He'd seen her gray eyes filled with lust and laughter, but never with fear. He'd kill the son of a bitch for putting that panic in her eyes.

But he couldn't do a damn thing duct taped to a chair in his own kitchen. Unable to move his feet away from the chair legs, he gripped the tile floor with his bare toes and curled them in an effort at forward motion. His thigh and calf muscles bunched, struggling to make it happen. His fingers gripped the chair arms so tight they turned white. The chair bobbled, but didn't move.

The phone rested on the counter three feet in front of him. Three. Fucking. Feet.

He clenched his toes again and wiggled his hips to shimmy the chair forward. Instead, it went backward a few inches.

Before frustration had a chance to burst to the forefront, the idea hit him. He wriggled only his right hip. Inch by inch, the chair turned so he faced the kitchen's bay window, dominated by the gloomy January sky and a large icicle dangling from the gutter. He ground his teeth together and concentrated all of his efforts on shuffling the chair back.

Left. Right. Left. Right. Left. Right. He passed the table.

With every inch he scooted, images of Josie at Snips' mercy bombarded him. Was she somewhere tied up? Were they on their way to the state line? Private planes landed at the Dry Creek Regional Airport all the time, what if Snips had one waiting on the runway? If that bastard hurt her in any way, Sam was going to tear him apart. Shit, he wanted to slam himself against a wall for not being able to stop the bastards.

The chair rammed into the counter. The phone stood near the counter's edge, just over his right shoulder, the red message light blinking.

Okay, he'd made it to the counter. Now what?

Panting, he sucked in some of the tape covering his mouth. The tape didn't tear at his lips. In fact, it wasn't sticking to them anymore. The mixture of saliva and blood had moistened the glue, making it ineffective.

He contorted his mouth under the tape, wetting as much of the underside as possible, then rubbing it against his shoulder. One corner came loose. Buoyed by the small success, he continued, ignoring the growing ache in his neck. After what seemed like eternity, the tape fell and hung limp from the corner of his mouth.

Sam shuffled a single hip again, turning the chair so the counter was to his right. He angled his head, arching his neck painfully, and knocked the phone from its base. It landed with a thunk against the granite and rolled three times before coming to rest half off the counter.

Fear squeezed his lungs, but the phone didn't fall. He exhaled and his shoulders relaxed. Leaning as far to the right as possible with the tape around his chest locking him to the chair, he reached for the phone with his mouth.

His shoulder bumped the counter.

The phone wavered on the edge, then plunged off.

For a millisecond, the world went blank.

Then the cool plastic fell into his hand and he wrapped his fingers around the phone. It took a second to regain control of his breathing and to clear the panic from his vision.

He inched the phone so his fingers could access the buttons and dialed nine-one-one.

"Dry Creek County Sheriff. What's your emergency?"

"This is Sam Layton. I'm at 1628 Pimlico Lane. There's been a kidnapping."

Fifteen minutes later, nearly every member of the Dry Creek County Sheriff's Office milled around in the street in front of his house. Half were there just to keep his mother from storming the place once she arrived. Inside the house was a different story. Only a handful of investigators gathered, conferring in quiet voices in the hall.

Bright red strips of raw skin crisscrossed his chest, arms and legs from where the paramedic had peeled the duct tape from his bare flesh. The same paramedic loomed over Sam, chewing her bottom lip.

"The nose is definitely broken." She shook her head, but not a single hair moved from her tight French braid. "It might take a couple of adjustments to get it in line. You sure you don't want to go the hospital and have the doc take a look?"

There wasn't time for the hospital. Josie was out there, in danger and alone. "Just do it."

She shrugged her shoulders and handed him a towel. "Blow your nose into this first."

Getting rid of the blood and muck stuffing his nose hurt like a son of a bitch, but he got it done and dropped the towel into the red bio-waste bag the paramedic held open.

"Okay, hold still, this will feel worse than having it broken in the first place." She put one latex-gloved hand on each side of his nose, her thumbs lined up against the swollen bridge. "So are there any Laytons who don't get beat up or shot?"

Before he could even formulate an answer, she pushed against his nose, forcing it back into place. Pain spiked through his sinuses.

The paramedic stepped back and cocked her head to one side. She hmmed a few times, then moved in for adjustment number two.

This time she didn't bother to distract him, just aligned her fingers against his nose and pushed. Another shot of agony exploded in his skull. She spread medical tape across his nose to hold it in place.

"Now you'll never be as pretty as me," Hank drawled from the doorway. "How's he doing?"

"Hey, Sheriff." The paramedic yanked off her gloves and tossed them in the red bag. "Ignoring advice to go to the hospital. That seems to be a thing with you Laytons."

Hank flashed the aw-shucks grin that had helped him win the last election. "Yeah, we can be real pains in the ass."

The paramedic rolled her eyes, grabbed her duffel bag of equipment and strode out of the kitchen, leaving Sam and his big brother alone.

Hank moved in front of him, standing arms akimbo. In his brown Dry Creek Sheriff's Office uniform, he looked all business.

But Sam didn't need the county sheriff right now. He needed the kind of backup only a brother could provide. He stood and a wave of dizziness and nausea made his empty stomach lurch. On automatic pilot, he grasped Hank's arm, anchoring himself to reality.

"Man, you probably have a concussion. You're going to the hospital."

Sam shook his head and tried to clear the fog clouding his mind. "They've got her."

"Who?"

"Some Vegas loan shark and his muscle took Josie and I couldn't do a damn thing to stop them." He dropped his hand to his side and tried to ignore the taste of vomit in his mouth.

Hank gave him the once over. "Looks like you sure as hell tried."

"Fat lot of good it did. Look, we don't have time to waste. We have to find her."

"Okay, start from the beginning and don't leave anything out."

By the time Sam had filled in all the blank spaces, he'd nearly paced a groove into the tile floor. "They took Josie and disappeared. They're either on their way to Vegas or using Josie to find Rebecca's Bounty."

"I've already called the airport. Deputies are all over the highways. If they're out there, we'll find them."

In his gut, Sam knew exactly where they'd taken Josie. "What if they're on McPherson's Bluff?"

"In this weather?" Hank glanced at the snowflakes dancing outside the bay window. "This is supposed to be just the beginning. If they're on the bluff, they'll be heading in soon. You stay here and I'll go take a look."

That was not going to happen. "I can't stay here. Josie's out there, Hank. What would you do if it was Beth?"

Hank's jaw tightened and a vein bulged in his temple. Only a few months ago, he and Beth had nearly been killed when they'd ended up in the middle of a deranged woman's revenge plot. The doctors declared he'd forever walk with a limp after taking a bullet in the knee to save Beth.

"You have two minutes to get some clothes on. I'll meet you at my cruiser."

# Chapter Sixteen

The darkness of the car trunk threatened to eat Josie up—or was that the anxiety talking?

"Get ahold of yourself, Winarsky. You're in a world of shit, yes, but that doesn't mean you don't have options."

Boxes and trash poked her on all sides. Something lay jammed underneath her rib cage. The trunk was a pit, there had to be a weapon in here somewhere. If she could just get her fingers wrapped around a tire iron or socket wrench, she wouldn't feel so helpless. Hopeless.

Josie pushed her legs out and arched her back. There wasn't enough room in the small, dark compartment to move more than an inch or two, but she managed to sweep her left hand across the floor, searching for anything she could use as a weapon. When Snips popped the lid, he'd be in for one hell of a surprise.

A square of plastic glowed above her. Outlined on it was the image of an open trunk.

An emergency release.

*Escape!*

Josie grabbed the corner, ready to yank, when the car veered off the smooth road and onto one so bumpy it bounced her off the floor and she banged her head on the trunk lid.

The car slowed.

Her blood pressure went up.

Frantic, she abandoned the escape release for the floor. Her fingers curled around something long and heavy with a cylindrical head. Socket wrench.

She clenched her jaw and began psyching herself up for Snips to open the trunk.

Another rut in the road sent the car jumping up again, but it kept bounding along. Figuring it was now or never, Josie yanked on the glowing square.

The trunk lid flew open.

Dawn's pink glow filled the sky, illuminating the empty countryside.

Sucking in a deep breath, Josie raised her arms to cover her head and rolled out of the trunk. All the air in her lungs vacated as soon as she landed with a thump on the dirt road.

The car kept moving.

She scrambled up, ignoring the blinding pain in her side, and stumbled to a copse of trees by an abandoned farmhouse. Rocks bit into her knees as she rested her forehead against scratchy bark, gulping in air and wondering how much time she had until Snips figured out she'd escaped.

Minutes. If she was lucky.

Her gaze followed her footprints between the road and her hiding spot. A dead giveaway. Careful as she could, she tiptoed in her tracks back to the road. The crusty top layer of snow stuck to her clammy palms when she tried to brush away evidence of her location. But the formerly powder snow had hardened during the cold night, making the top layer as brittle as the crust on a crème brûlée.

She searched the area but everywhere she looked, the light gleamed off the icy covering. Despite the cold, a bead of sweat rolled down the back of her neck.

That's when she saw it. Under the trees, the snow had piled up into a small mound, no doubt pushed by the winds that never ceased to blow.

Josie negotiated her way back to the trees as quickly as she could while not making any new footprints, gathered an armful of snow and scurried back to the road. She packed the fresh snow into the indentations left by her boots, smoothing it as best she could, and working her way backwards until the evergreens blocked her from the road.

Her breath hovered in the air as she panted. She rubbed away the goose bumps that had grown into goose mountains on her arms and tried to formulate a plan.

At the rumble of a car's engine, her first instinct was to spring from her hiding spot and wave down the motorist. She caught herself just in time. Peeking through the branches, she watched a sedan with Nevada plates crawl down the dirt road.

Blood roared in her ears and she double-checked the job she'd done with the snow. Dread squeezed her throat closed. Quarter-sized drops of red spotted the path between where she'd landed in the road and the tree line. She wiped her hand across her lower back where the trunk had snagged her skin and stared down at red-tipped fingers. The cold and her own panic had blunted the pain, but hadn't stopped the bleeding.

The black vehicle continued forward. Too late. Nothing she could do but cross her fingers and hope.

Josie squeezed her legs close to her chest, wrapping her arms around her shins.

The engine's purr was practically next to her now.

She clenched her eyes shut and buried her face between her knees.

"Josie girl, we're going to find you." The wind carried Snips' taunting call across the frozen fields and giant snowflakes fell from the sky.

Every nerve in her body screamed at her to push away from the tree's rough bark and run. To sprint to safety.

But there was no haven out here, only flat, snowy land until McPherson's Bluff rose straight and tall from the plains half a mile away—or the decrepit farmhouse ten yards ahead.

Muscles tensed, she waited. Trapped.

Just when she thought she couldn't take it anymore, the motor of Snips' car faded away.

Too freaked out to be relieved, she forced herself to count to one hundred to make sure they'd gone before hurrying to the farmhouse to assess her options in a more protected area.

Someone had nailed two-by-fours across the windows and doorway. She yanked at the boards covering the door until one finally gave way, providing just enough room for her to crawl through. Dirt and trash covered the floor. Twigs and bits of debris formed what looked like a nest inside the hearth. She scanned the room for occupants. The last thing she needed was a rabid animal thinking she'd invaded its turf. Finding nothing, Josie sank to the floor, wanting nothing more in the world than to fall apart.

She ground her teeth together, determined to stave off anxious tears. Fuck this. If there was any time to reach down deep and proudly wear her pair of brass balls, this was it. She inhaled a deep breath of frigid air and let it out in a huff.

Better. She could do this.

৯৯৯৯

Sam clicked his seat belt and clutched Josie's new, Nebraska-winter-worthy coat in his lap. No doubt she'd be freezing once they found her.

The snowfall had gained intensity in the ten minutes he and Hank had been on the road. Wind pushed against the cruiser and swirled the quarter-inch of snow covering the asphalt. McPherson's Bluff towered over the prairie, an optical illusion making is seem just around the bend when in reality it was a good fifteen miles away.

"So Chris tells me Josie is a waitress in Vegas."

"Yes. She's a painter too."

"Any good?"

Guilt sucker-punched him in the kidneys. "I don't know, I haven't seen any of her paintings." He'd spent so much time questioning her motives or trying to get into her pants, he hadn't bothered to find out more about the one thing that really mattered to her.

*You're a real asshole, Layton.*

"So should we try the east or west entrance to the bluff?"

"Neither, we have to start at the beginning. They took both maps. I marked the regional map with the possible beginnings. They have to know the starting point is either Rebecca's first homestead or the McNerny boarding house."

Hank gave him a hearty dose of side eye. "Dial that back, professor, and talk to me like I don't live this crap every day."

"Sorry. Snips is after Rebecca's Bounty. That's why my office was trashed this week. He told Josie that if she finds the treasure for him, he'll forget he wants to turn her brother over to some mob boss."

Hank's mouth gaped open, but he kept his eyes on the ever-worsening road. When he didn't say anything, Sam shrugged and continued.

"Josie was given Rebecca's diary. Inside the back cover was a map to the treasure. The key to finding it is knowing the correct place to start, homestead or boarding house."

"So which is it?" Hank rolled to a stop at a T in the road.

Go left to the west side of the bluff and Rebecca's first homestead. Go right to the east side of the bluff and the McNerny boarding house. He had a fifty-fifty chance of getting it right, if he was correct about Snips' determination to get the treasure. With Josie's life on the line, he had to be.

"Turn left." The sky had turned white and visibility had gone from so-so to downright concerning. They were the only vehicle on the two-lane highway. "Thanks for doing this, Hank."

"Better than just taking off, which you would have done about ten minutes after I'd left you alone."

"True."

"At least this way if we get stranded in the middle of a snowstorm, Mom won't kill me for letting you go off on your own."

"You'd think we were still kids the way she mother-bears us."

"Yeah, I think we're forever twelve to her."

Sam couldn't help but wince at the mention of being twelve, especially with McPherson's Bluff taking up a big portion of the real estate in front of the windshield.

Ever observant, Hank didn't miss a thing. "Shit, Sam. I'm sorry."

"I think it's time we moved beyond that—way past time when I need to do that."

He rubbed the fleece lining of Josie's electric-blue coat between his thumb and finger. They'd find her and then he'd find the words to tell her everything. He couldn't promise forever, but he sure could do a damn sight better about the here and the now.

Despite the weather conditions, Hank made good time, turning onto Rural Route Fourteen without having to sacrifice much in terms of speed for the dirt road. The cruiser's shocks absorbed most of the beating from the rough surface. Three miles in and they were almost to the trees Rebecca had used as a windbreak for her new home.

There wasn't much left of Rebecca's original homestead, but five years ago the Dry Creek Historical Society had started to build a replica of the one-room farmhouse. They'd gotten about halfway through the building process when funds ran out, the economy tanked and donations dried up. The abandoned building stood alone just off the road.

He searched the road ahead for tire tracks, but the fresh layer of snow, now at least a half-inch thick, covered any sign of previous traffic.

"Pull over by the trees."

Hank put the car in park. "Okay, we treat this as a possible crime scene. You stay behind me and if I tell you to get back to the car, you get the fuck back. Agreed?"

"Agreed."

The frigid air slapped Sam in the face as soon as he climbed out of the cruiser, chapping his cheeks. Josie would be freezing out here in just jeans and a T-shirt. He could still feel the soft cotton under his fingers. Had that only been a few hours ago? God, it seemed like forever.

He fell in line behind Hank, who crept toward the white clapboard house with his gun drawn.

Wind whipped across the open field, blowing flakes and making the house seem more like a mirage than a reality.

Adrenaline-spiked blood pumped at hyper-speed through Sam's system and despite the cold, the small of his back grew damp with sweat.

లలల

Josie's fingers had turned white from the cold without gloves or coat pockets to protect them. She rubbed them together, pain pricking down their lengths as the blood returned. Outside the snowfall grew denser.

Once frostbite stopped being an immediate concern, she took inventory. One socket wrench. Her car keys. The pay-as-you-go cellphone Cy had given her. She flipped it open. No bars. Of course not, that would have made getting the hell out of here too damn easy.

She stood and extended the arm holding the phone high above her head the circled the room. In the corner closest to the animal nest, one of the bars flickered to life, then went dark. Willing circumstances to change, Josie crossed the room. No luck.

The phone snapped closed with a click and she slid it into her back pocket. She hunkered down by her other weapons. She balanced the socket wrench in her hand. Heavy, solid. It felt good. That would add some umph to her right hook.

Feet crunched on the icy snow outside of the boarded-up window.

As soundlessly as she could, she backed into a dark corner, gripping her makeshift weapons in each hand. Predator or rescuer, one wrong move and he was going to get a mouth full of metal.

Gloved fingers wrapped around a board blocking up the door and yanked it free.

જન્જન્

They were within two feet of the front door when a high-pitched cry broke the silence and a blur of light gray burst from the homestead's front door.

The coyote ran serpentine around Sam and Hank before breaking into a straight run across the flat land and disappearing into the snow.

Hank recovered first and started back toward the house. He disappeared inside the doorway and returned a moment later, his eyes downcast.

Fear bristled along Sam's spine. Were they too late? He sprinted to the door and pushed past Hank.

His gaze traveled the darkened expanse of the room, searching each shadow for Josie's bright platinum curls.

Nothing.

Dread filled him and threatened to knock him to his knees. Damn Rebecca and her treasure.

*There is a beauty to this hard land more valuable than treasure, but for those who insist, I give you this*, she'd written.

Sam stumbled outside and into the vast shadow of McPherson's Bluff. Oh yes, it was beautiful in the same way a cobra about to strike could be breathtaking.

He tried to hold on to hope, to the belief that this time he would be able to save a life. He pushed away the doubts, but like a spurned, angry lover, they refused to leave.

Hank clapped a hand on Sam's shoulder, displacing some of the snow piled there. "Don't worry, we'll find her."

But would they? And if so, would they be in time?

# Chapter Seventeen

ell, Josie girl, I told you we'd find you." Snips stepped through the gap between boards nailed across the empty door. "And to think we found you right where we wanted to stop in the first place. I told you we went too far, Linc."

A shadow moved in front of the partially boarded-up doorway, which Josie assumed belonged to Linc. The muscle man must be too big to fit through the opening. Who would have thought the big man's size would finally work to her advantage?

She gripped the socket wrench tight in her left hand, held at an angle behind her back. She curled her right hand into a fist and rested it against her thigh. Surprise would only be on her side once and she'd need it to knock out Snips. The steroids had shrunk his balls but they'd also pumped up his muscles and temper. Of course with the amount of pissed-off adrenaline pumping through her veins, she figured she still had the upper hand. She'd flatten him. Then she'd have to get past Linc in the doorway, which wasn't as likely to be successful unless she timed it just right.

"What, no smart remark this time?" Snips strutted closer.

Josie barely kept the instinct to swing wildly at him in check. Like a poker player, she needed to stay calm, keep emotion out of it and wait for the perfect time to make her move.

"I think I like you better now that you've finally shut the fuck up. You ready to play ball?" He was almost within reach now.

Just another step closer.

He stopped and raised an eyebrow. "Whatever you're cookin', Josie girl, you better just give it up." His left hand whipped out and he backhanded her across the cheek.

The metallic taste of blood filled her mouth.

"That should make sure you keep your smart mouth shut."

Josie spit the mouthful of blood to the floor, splattering Snips' snow-covered boots. "Not even close."

She smacked the smirk off his face with an uppercut to the jaw with her right fist, followed by a haymaker utilizing the socket wrench in her left. The silver cylinder cracked against Snips' jaw and he went down hard.

"Mr. Esposito, you okay in there?" Linc peered through the slits between the boards. "What's going on in there?"

Snips moaned out an unintelligible response.

Linc wrapped his meaty fingers around a two-by-four and yanked.

Blackness ate into the edges of Josie's line of sight and she couldn't catch her breath.

A chunk of sky appeared in the doorway and Linc reached for the next board. Two more and he'd be able to squeeze in.

Motivated by a desperate need to live another day, she patted down Snips' pants, looking for a gun, a knife, anything. She came up empty.

Another board hit the floor.

Her blood pressure spiked.

Josie sprinted to the hearth and gathered as much dirt and twigs from the animal nest as she could. She made it back to the doorway a half second after Linc tore the last board from the wall.

Without giving herself time to doubt, she tossed the debris in Linc's face.

He cried out in shock and slapped his hands to his eyes.

Before he had a chance to wipe the grime away, Josie took off out the front door. Her boots slapped across the porch and down the creaky steps. The world was awash in white, making it impossible to tell which way led back to Dry Creek and which farther into the sticks. She hit the snow-covered ground, cranked up her speed and shot toward McPherson's Bluff.

"You better find a damn good hiding place, girlie," Snips shouted. "Because when I find you, you're going to pay with that pretty ass of yours."

Josie heeded his warning and ran. The air burned her lungs from the inside out and every snap of frigid wind against her bare arms reminded her of just how long she'd been out in the elements without a coat or gloves. *The pain beat being dead.*

In better conditions and with actual running shoes, she'd clear the half mile to McPherson's Bluff in about five minutes. But with every step, her boots sank in the snow. The wind and snow picked up, bringing visibility to a few feet beyond arm's reach. Her chattering teeth had overtaken the wind's howl in the noise contest. After a few minutes, she wasn't so sure she wouldn't be better off numb.

But she tucked her chin into her chest and pushed forward. Every few steps, she glanced over her shoulder to see if Snips and Linc were on her trail. She couldn't see them or the abandoned house anymore. However, her danger detector hadn't stopped blaring a warning siren, so she continued with one foot in front of the other until she came to the bluff's base.

Rising eight hundred feet from the prairie, it stood tall and proud, unbent by time or the weather. The damn thing reminded her of Sam. When she'd left him, he'd been hurt but alive. If she could keep Snips and Linc following her, they wouldn't be able to return to Dry Creek to torment Sam.

"You still out there you shithead, Snips?" she hollered in the direction of the abandoned house. "You better find me before I find you because one of us isn't coming out of here alive."

Not that she had any weapons to back up that threat since she'd left the socket wrench in the cabin, but since when did bravado require a strong sense of reality? Warmed with defiance, she took off around the bluff, looking for a place to hide or a path to take. She crossed her arms and shoved her hands into her armpits as great shivers racked her body. The snow had begun to slow, but the temperature hadn't left the freezing zone. She had to find somewhere to hide out quick, or hypothermia would get her before Snips ever did.

The snow disguised any easy path up the bluff. She'd trudged past the four-foot high triangle-shaped boulder twice before its meaning connected with her foggy brain. Rebecca's map had shown a similar formation next to a path. At the moment she didn't give a damn about the treasure, but a place to bury Rebecca's Bounty could make the perfect hiding place from the wind and the men chasing her.

Another blast of wind smacked against her body, burning her with cold. Damp hair stuck to her neck and forehead. Her ears ached with pinpricks of agony as her veins constricted in her extremities to retain heat in her core. Tears sprung to her eyes, not of sadness or fright but of pain. Snow had found its way into her boots during the run and melted, turning her socks to wet cloth.

She had to move. Now.

Her mind urged her body to scramble up the incline to the triangle bolder, but her legs were mired in molasses. The distance to the four-foot-high rock seemed miles. But she hadn't come this far to lie down and wait for Snips to do his worst.

One boot-clad foot clomped in front of the other as she made her way upward. With nothing to hold on to, she slipped on the wet snow a few times but managed to fight her way to the bolder. Climbing the two-foot incline zapped more of her energy than it should have and she leaned her back against Rebecca's landmark. Icy snow soaked through her T-shirt along her spine, from the small of her back to between her shoulder blades, and another set of shivers shook her.

She glanced around, hoping to find a nice little cabin with smoke billowing from the fireplace. No such luck. The only things she spotted were rocks and a few pine trees covered in white. A natural path had been worn in the stone bluff from centuries of people traveling across it, curving around into what she couldn't see. Well, she knew full well what kind of trouble followed behind her so she might as well go forward.

Josie marched on, too exhausted and cold to worry about the tracks she left in the snow. The path's slope grew steeper and she had to lean forward as she walked. Higher and higher she went, passing snow-covered rocks and trees, but not finding anything that would offer protection from the wind. At least the snow had stopped. Thank God for small favors.

By now, her body twitched with cold on an almost constant basis and she'd begun to lose hope of ever finding a safe spot to stop. The bluff's limestone walls went straight up on the right. On the left, the landscape dropped in a steep slope to a badlands of deep ravines. Looking out at the blanket of white as far as she could see, she couldn't help but remember Rebecca's words. There was a harsh beauty to this place. If it didn't turn you into a human Popsicle first.

Bringing her gaze back down to the snowy path, she forced herself to keep moving. Her pace had slowed to the speed of an eighty-year-old crossing the road, but she was making progress. As a bonus, the frosty temperature didn't bother the white tips on her fingers anymore.

A few minutes, hours or days later—really, she'd lost all ability to track time—she passed into a deep shadow. She blinked a few times in response to the light change and glanced up. A slab of rock crossed above the path, creating a land bridge from one part of the bluff to another.

A fuzzy picture formed in her mind. A sketch. Had she painted a similar formation? No. Rebecca. It was the third or fourth drawing on the map. Somehow, she'd stumbled upon it.

She pressed her back against the limestone wall and looked up at the rock, her entire body weary.

With no destination in mind, would it really matter if she took a short rest? Her eyelids drooped. Just for a couple of minutes of shuteye and then she'd get moving again.

Darkness surrounded her and sank into her bones. Everything became heavy. She was going to die out here, only to be found by some hiker in the spring. What a fucking way to go. Maybe she should have taken her chances with Snips. *Too late for second-guessing now*.

Even the effort to stay upright proved too much and she slid down the hard limestone wall. Rocks shook loose behind her, showering her shoulders with chunks of the chalky limestone.

The wall crashed around her and Josie tumbled back into a small cave, landing flat on her back.

The impact knocked the breath out of her frozen lungs and jarred to the surface the pain that had been waiting just under the numbness. Agony pierced her skin and she curled into the fetal position in an instinctual attempt to block it all out.

Desperate to think about anything but the stabbing pain, she forced herself to take in her surroundings. If this qualified as a cave, it was the studio apartments of caves. It was so small she could reach out and touch both walls at the same time. It ended about eight feet back from the entrance, where the two walls came together to form a V.

Mercifully, the wind couldn't penetrate beyond the cave's mouth. Maybe if she was lucky, Snips would find her soon. Right about now, she'd pick him over freezing to death. She snorted, sending a puff of dust into the air. *Well, if that right there doesn't tell you you're fucked, then nothing does.*

Josie rolled over to her stomach. She half crawled, half slid to the back of the cave.

A small, intricately carved wood box the length of a business envelope lay nestled in the corner. An ornate R stood out on the lid.

Rebecca's Bounty.

So many people had searched for the treasure and she'd found it. Now she'd die with it.

Resigned to her fate, she sat up, pulled her legs to her chest and curled her upper body downward, trapping her hands and Rebecca's Bounty between her thighs and boobs. The V of the walls coming together fit snug against her shoulders and she let herself loosen her tenuous hold on reality. If she was going to embark on that final adventure, she might as well go happy.

Relaxing into herself, she imagined it was Sam holding her tight, whispering her name into the nape of her neck. The blackness came again, eating at the edges of her vision. Too tired to fight it anymore, she closed her eyes and surrendered.

The howling wind became silent.

Her breathing slowed.

The beating in her chest grew soft.

Her fantasy lover warmed her with his strong arms and she pressed her icy cheek against his welcoming chest. God, he smelled of warm leather and old books. She wrapped her arms around his waist, tucking her hands into his waistband above his firm ass. Even in this in-between place, she couldn't let go of Sam.

Sam stared out at the white-covered fields as Hank's cruiser crawled down the highway toward the original McNerny boarding house, hampered by the fast-falling snow. All that was left was a historical marker, but there was an old farmhouse nearby. There was a good chance Snips had taken Josie there to wait out the storm. Whereever she was, they'd find her. They had to.

"Sheriff, the state patrol is closing down the Interstate," a voice crackled on the police radio.

Hank cursed under his breath and grabbed the radio mic. "How many of our folks are still on the highways, Darlene?"

"All of them. Phillips just reported the southern sections of the county are getting hit hard. How is it up north where you are?"

"It's as white as a fridge out here."

"Any luck tracking down our perps?"

"I haven't given up yet. Any reports from the others?"

"Negative."

Sam slid a glance over at Hank. He held a white-knuckle grip on the steering wheel with one hand, battling the slippery road. Sam's stomach clenched. He had to find Josie, but could he risk his brother's life to do so? McPherson's Bluff loomed a half mile away, like a nightmare Sam couldn't wake up from no matter how many times he pinched himself. He'd already lost one brother in the shadow of the bluff. He couldn't live with himself if he lost another.

"Hank, why don't you have one of your guys meet us out here? He can take you back and I'll continue the search."

"We'll find her, Sam."

"But you—"

"I said, we'll find her." Hank said. "Darlene, tell the others to get back to Dry Creek. It's getting too dangerous out."

"Ten-four. You on your way back?"

Hank shook his head. "No. We're checking out the old McNerny boarding house. I'll be in touch."

"Yes sir."

Neither man spoke as the wind whipped snow all around them and rocked the car from its straight-and-narrow path. Everything that needed to be said was being delivered by the invisible brother bond that didn't require words.

"What's that up there?" Hank nodded toward a black square on the horizon.

Sam squinted, trying to make it out. His gut twitched. "I think it's a car."

The black spot grew in their windshield, until no doubt remained. Snips' car sat parked by a grove of trees near a small farmhouse. Sam's heartbeat ratcheted up and he barely controlled the urge to leap from the still-moving cruiser to search for Josie.

The sedan's tires spit white powder from the ground as it rolled out onto the highway, coming straight at them.

Hank steered the cruiser into the middle of the road. "Hold on." He spun the steering wheel, whipping the car perpendicular to the highway, blocking the escape.

The other car bore down on them, never wavering from its dead-on trajectory.

The yards between them became feet in a blink of Sam's eye. In his next heartbeat, the other car plowed into the back passenger side of the cruiser, throwing him forward against the seatbelt. It tightened across his neck, cutting off his oxygen as blinding pain exploded in his right arm.

Everything whirled around him as the cruiser spun across the highway in a death spin. His lungs tightened, pushed back against his spine by the strength of the rotations. The cruiser sailed off the highway and into the snow-covered field. The revolutions slowed until the vehicle came to a stop, McPherson's Bluff towering above him.

A crash boomed in the distance, followed by a bright light that turned the milky sky orange.

Sam stumbled from the cruiser, his boots sinking in the powdery snow. Blood dripped from a deep gash in his biceps, falling in fat drops and staining the blanket of white at his feet.

Across the highway, Snips' car had barreled through the copse of trees, mowed over the historical marker and burst into a fireball.

"Josie!" His anguished cry thundered across the prairie as he took off in a mad dash toward the bonfire of metal and the sickly scent of burning flesh.

A wall of heat stopped him from getting within ten feet of the burning wreckage. No one could make it out of there alive.

Sam dropped to his knees as true agony ripped his soul in half. He should have fought more. He should have stopped this. He should have been smarter about how to track her down. What kind of man couldn't save the woman he loved?

The kind who didn't deserve her.

"There's someone over here." Hank called from the other side of the flames.

He bounded up from the road, sprinting to his brother's side.

Snips' mangled, bloody body lay in the snow.

The Vegas loan shark blinked up at the two men. "Help...me."

A rage unlike anything he'd ever known overtook Sam. "You killed her, you bastard!"

He wrapped his hands around Snips' throat, channeling all of his fury into the act of squeezing the life out of the man who'd stolen the woman he loved. His fingers dug into the muscles of Snips' neck, pushing against the bones of his trachea.

Snips gasped and squirmed under the pressure, but Sam held on. If he couldn't save Josie, he sure as hell would avenge her.

"Stop!" Hank bellowed into his ear and pried him away from his prey.

Sam landed with a thump on his ass in the snow and bounded up immediately. Hank stood, palms facing outward, blocking his return. Enraged, Sam fought to get close enough to strangle the life out of Snips, but Hank ran interference, knocking him on his ass three times.

But he refused to give up; he'd failed her too many times already to mess up this one final thing.

The brothers grappled, elbows and fists flying. Sam hooked Hank into a headlock, holding firm, and leaned down to his ear. "She's burning up in that car because of him, Hank! I'm going to kill him. Just walk away."

"Not...dead," Snips croaked out from the ground. "She ran...to the bluff."

"I'm not buying it, you lying sack of shit."

Hank wriggled out of the headlock. "If she did, she had to have left tracks. Let's go look, you and me. This asshole isn't going anywhere."

Calling a temporary truce, the brothers made their way across the road, searching for footprints, starting near where the cruiser had come to rest. Sam almost walked right on top of a size-ten boot print. He held his breath and closed his eyes, praying to God when he opened them that the indentation in the snow would still be there.

It was.

"I found it."

"Let me call it in, we'll organize a search party." Hank reached inside the cruiser for the police radio. "The snow has slowed so we have time."

Sam glanced over at the cruiser's open door. He could see Josie's new winter coat sitting on the seat and fear flattened his chest. "No time. I'm going now."

"Sam, wait!"

There wasn't any time to wait. Josie was out there.

# Chapter Eighteen

$\mathcal{S}$am trailed Josie's tracks to the base of McPherson's Bluff. The snow had tapered off, leaving only the wind whacking at his body like an icy hand. He raised the zipper on his heavy coat to ward off Mother Nature's attack.

Scanning the bluff, he searched for her platinum hair and the all-black outfit she'd worn to break into his house, grateful her sense of drama would make her stand out in the all-white environment. Seeing nothing, he followed her footprints, noting how they grew closer together and in some spots they were broken where she must have fallen. A perfect handprint broke through the snow near a bolder. An image of her bare hand, red with cold, flashed in his mind.

It had to be five degrees out and she didn't have a coat or gloves. How long had she been wandering around the bluff and how much longer could she take the freezing temperatures? The question pierced him like a bull's horns, guilt-filled pain spreading outward. He pushed back the anxiety curling around his heart. Later, after he had her warm and in his arms, he'd deal with that. For now, he just had to find her.

Josie's tracks circled around in an aimless pattern the farther up the bluff he went. A large dent in the snowpack was evidence that she'd fallen at least one more time. Sirens blared in the distance. The sheriff's deputies, fire department and ambulance, no doubt. The cavalry had arrived too late.

Halfway up to the top of the bluff's eight-hundred-feet summit, the tracks disappeared near a steep drop-off. Blood rushed in his ears, drowning out the sirens, and he ran to the edge and looked into the abyss. Evergreen trees broke through the undisturbed white blanket like polka dots between the bluff and the badlands' deep ravines beyond, but no black clothing to give away Josie.

He whipped around, looking for more tracks. Nothing but a haphazard scattering of large rocks near a two-foot crack in the limestone wall broke up the perfect blanket of white. Rockslide. Those were usually a problem in the spring, not the dead of winter. An animal must have—

Adrenaline electrified his body and he rushed to the opening. He couldn't see anything in the inky blackness, but part of him knew, just knew, she was in there.

"Josie, I'm coming for you." His voice echoed back at him.

The cave was so narrow the walls brushed against both his shoulders in some areas, pointed rocks snagging the nylon of his coat and poking the gash in his upper arm. His eyes adjusted to the dim interior. A small mound of black was in the back corner. He couldn't make it out at first—then he noticed the blonde curls.

Sam rushed over and dropped to his knees beside her still form. Her already pale skin had turned ghostly white. He gathered her up in his arms, begging God for her life. A pulse, slow and erratic, beat against her neck.

"It's okay, I've got you. You're going to be okay. We'll get you warmed up and you'll be right as rain," he babbled into her hair as he unzipped his coat. "You just have to hang on for me a little bit longer."

He brought her frigid body against his chest, brought the edges of his coat around her back and wrapped his arms around her. She clutched a small box in her hands, unwilling to let go even in her unconscious state. She was so cold, her forehead burned his neck when she rested it against him. Sam scooped her up, a firebrand of pain searing through his injured arm. He flinched and backed out of the cave as carefully as possible.

The trip down McPherson's Bluff and across the field to the ambulance went by in a blur. Snips was already on the stretcher, but the paramedics rushed over to Sam.

The paramedic took her pulse and gave her a quick check. "She's probably got hypothermia; we need to get her to the hospital right away."

"We can take her in the cruiser," Hank said. "Sam, get in the back with her. Keep her warm."

Sam laid Josie down in the back seat and ripped off his coat. He slid in beside her, pulled her cold body onto his lap and covered her with his coat like a blanket. Sam hadn't prayed since before Michael died, but for the second time that afternoon, he begged God to save Josie's life. She shivered in his arms and he continued to bargain and plead, offering everything he had so she could live.

Hank sped down the country road and flipped on the sirens once they hit the highway. As soon as they pulled up to the emergency entrance, a team of hospital staff streamed out of the double doors. An orderly yanked open the door, pulled Josie from Sam's arms and whisked her away on a stretcher.

He tried to follow, but Hank's hand on his shoulder stilled him. "They'll take care of her, don't worry."

๛๛๛

Sam paced the hospital waiting room, which was crowded with Laytons. Chris and Hank huddled in one corner with Hank's girlfriend, Beth Martinez, sending him sympathetic looks over their coffee cups. After the nurse had warned them they were in for a long wait, Claire and her fiancé, Jake Warrick, had gone to her restaurant, Harvest, to bring back food, but they'd be back soon. His parents, Glenda and Bob, maintained a silent vigil in the center of the room.

"Samuelson Aaron Layton, come sit down by me." Glenda patted the empty lime-green chair. "The doctor said you lost quite a bit of blood before she stitched you up and you won't do Josie a bit of good if you pass out cold."

He glanced down at the white bandage circling his biceps. Fifteen stitches. Josie might be dying and his mom worried about him passing out?

Heat flushed his cheeks and anger at his own impotence expanded in his chest like a hot-air balloon. Ugly words formed in his mind, but before they could leave his mouth, he saw the worry heavy in her tear-swollen eyes. The fury deflated in an instant and he shuffled over to the seat.

Glenda slid her hand into his and squeezed. "She'll make it, don't you worry about Josie."

The door swung open and a doctor walked in. The already high tension level rocketed as everyone in the room focused on the tired man in front of them.

"I'm Dr. Coll. Have you been able to locate Ms. Winarsky's family yet?"

"Not yet." Hank rubbed the back of his neck, remembering the frustration of finding only one contact number in her phone. "We left a message for her brother."

Coll consulted his clipboard. "I see." He stood silent for three long breaths before gazing back up and focusing on Sam. "Miss Winarsky is suffering from hypothermia, but we're bringing her core temperature back up and she's on a thiamine and glucose drip."

The pressure in Sam's chest eased and he took the first deep, calm breath since Snips had knocked him unconscious this morning.

"However, there are complications." The doctor paused, letting the revelation sink in. "She has frostbite in four of her fingers on the right hand. With this level of injury, the muscles, blood vessels, nerves and tendons in her fingers froze."

Tension pulled his spine straight. "Will you have to amputate?"

"Not right now. We like to take a wait-and-see approach to frostbite injuries such as this. Most likely, nerve damage will be the worst she has to contend with."

"And without that luck?" Sam hated to have to ask the question.

The doctor chomped on his gum and the grooves in his forehead deepened. "At worst there could be permanent numbness in those fingers and we may even have to amputate—but those cases are rare. She should be fine in a few weeks."

"But she's a painter, if she can't use her fingers, how will she work?" After all she'd gone through and the sacrifices she'd made to paint, the news would devastate her.

"I'm afraid I can't answer that. She'll need to stay here for the next few days so we can monitor her heart for irregularity and treat the frostbite." Dr. Coll turned and opened the door. "We just have to hope for the best."

"Can I see her?"

The doctor shook his head. "Not until we get her core temperature to where it should be. Go home and get some rest."

With that final bit of advice, Dr. Coll turned and left the room.

Shell-shocked, Sam couldn't move from his chair. His family gathered around him, offering the silent support of their presence.

"Why don't you come on home with us tonight, I'll make some mac and cheese and you can sleep in your old room." His mother patted his knee.

Just the idea of leaving Josie felt like an additional betrayal. Even if he couldn't be with her, he wouldn't let her be alone again. "No, I'm staying."

ഔഔഔ

It was close to midnight when the hospital waiting room's taupe walls starting closing in on Sam. His mother and father had nodded off in their chairs. Everyone else had gone home for some shuteye hours ago. A jittery edginess had invaded his muscles and he needed to move. He'd take a quick trip to the cafeteria and see if there was a vending machine or coffee.

The wide hallway was deserted at this hour, but a group of women gathered at the nurses' station at the end of the hall. A woman laughed and Sam recognized the voice. Keely dePaul was the only woman he knew with such a husky laugh, made even deeper by the cigarette habit she'd had since they went to high school.

"Hey, Keely, can I talk to you a minute?"

Her gaze soft with sympathy, the same look half the town had given him when Michael died, she nodded and took a few steps away from the other women dressed in light-blue scrubs.

"How you holding up?"

"I'll live." He flinched at his own words. "I need to see her."

Keely glanced around. "Follow me."

Their steps echoed off the walls as he followed her down the hallway. She passed five doors before stopping and opening one.

Josie lay on the bed covered in blankets and heat lamps circled her bed, making the temperature in the room warmer than it was in the rest of hospital. A heart monitor beeped in a steady rhythm next to the bed. Her face was swollen, and thick white bandages wrapped around the fingers on her right hand. He took a step into the room, but Keely's hand on his arm stopped him from going in farther.

"You can't touch her. We've raised her temperature and given her pain medication, but her skin is very sensitive. Imagine the pain of the pins-and-needles feeling when your leg falls asleep and multiply it times a million."

"Will she be okay?" Just asking the question was like standing on the edge of the world knowing a strong breeze could blow him over and into oblivion.

"She's strong, Sam. Her heart is responding well and she reacted well to the rewarming protocol. I can't make any promises, but the outlook is good. Try not to wake her up."

Focused only on the woman in the bed, Sam didn't even realize Keely was leaving until the door clicked shut behind him. For once, Josie looked small and fragile, lying on the bed connected to an IV and heart monitor. The sight nearly killed him.

It was more than just a sense of failed responsibility. It was love. He'd known there was something special about her the moment he sat down at that bar in Vegas. Smart, vivacious and sexy as hell, Josie woke him up from a life of settling for good enough and made him want to be a better man, the kind of man she deserved.

"I promise I'll do whatever it takes to be that man." His voice cracked and he dropped his face into his hands.

Tears wet his palms, the first he'd cried since Michael had died. Instead of stuffing the emotion back into a dark box, he let it go and his shoulders shook under the weight of his silent anguish.

# Chapter Nineteen

*S*oft beeps invaded Josie's subconscious, pulling her from the heavy sleep. She blinked her eyes open and white filled her view. How had the snow gotten into the cave?

Her vision focused and she realized the white above her were ceiling tiles. The cold that had seeped into her bones had disappeared, replaced by a lethargy that numbed her body.

Once the strong odor of disinfectant pierced her consciousness, she recalled waking up in the hospital yesterday. The forced-air warming blankets they'd used to defrost her and the desperate yearning for Sam had been the first things she'd felt upon regaining consciousness yesterday afternoon.

Early morning sunlight filtered in through the partially closed blinds. It danced in lines across the white blanket covering most of her body. A needle stuck out from a vein on top of her left hand, connected by a tube to a bag of clear fluids.

She turned her head and there was Sam.

He was asleep in a chair across the room, his body twisted into an awkward position with his chin resting on his chest. His broad shoulders rose and fell in a steady rhythm.

"Sam." Her voice sounded raw as she called out to him.

His head snapped up, tawny eyes wide. For the span of three beeps from the EKG machine monitoring her heart, they just gazed at each other. Josie never thought she'd see him again and relief rushed through her.

He jumped up from his seat and knelt beside the bed. "Josie, I'm so sorry. I should have stopped them. I should have found you sooner."

"Shut up, Sam."

His hazel eyes widened and his shoulders sagged. The idiot thought she was going to kick him to the curb.

"The only thing I thought about while I was on the run was doing whatever it took to keep them away from you. That was the most important thing in the world to me." The light from the heat lamps surrounding her bed turned his hair into the color of a hot July sunset and she wished like hell she could touch him.

Before he could say anything, the door slammed open.

Cy, dressed in head-to-toe black, took up almost the entire space. A petite woman stood just behind him.

"Hey there, little brother."

Cy strode into the room, stopping just shy of Sam, who quickly stood up. Not bothering to look at the other man, Cy kept his focus on her and completed a slow perusal of her battered body, taking stock of each minor scrape and major injury. By the time he reached her toes, an angry flush burned in his cheeks. The brunette slipped her hand into Cy's and squeezed.

"I'm going to kill that shithead Snips," he bit out.

"He's down the hall with a police guard in front of his door, but I wouldn't bother. The doctors don't expect him to pull through." Josie shrugged her shoulders, the small movement sending waves of pain rippling through her body. "Anyway, you'll have to stand in line behind Sam and me to get a crack at him."

At this, Cy turned his attention toward Sam. He puffed out his chest and took half a step closer. "My sister is in this hospital because of you."

Sam said nothing but the vein in his temple went into overdrive.

A heat wave swept through her body. "Cy, that's not fair."

"Not fair?" he roared. "You almost freeze to death while this yahoo and his brother meandered about. Hell, if they hadn't lucked into finding Snips' car, you'd be a block of ice by now."

"Stop being an asshole, Cy—"

"No, he's right." Sam turned his hazel gaze on her. "I failed you."

An ache started in her chest, making her throat close and her eyes water. If someone had ripped out her lungs from her chest, Josie couldn't have hurt more than she did at that moment.

When she opened her mouth to speak, he stopped her with an upraised palm. "Let me finish."

She nodded, her heart fluttering.

Sam glanced at their company and the tips of his ears turned magenta. He drummed his fingertips against the outside of his thighs and chewed his bottom lip before refocusing all his attention on her. The self-conscious tension melted out of his shoulders. "You are exactly what I never realized I needed in my life. You're fun and adventurous and you wouldn't know how to go along to get along if you had an instruction manual. You make me want to be a better man. The kind of man who deserves you."

The ability to form words deserted Josie and she stared dumbfounded at him. She needed to say something—anything—but her mind had gone completely blank.

"I'll leave now." A wicked look darkened Sam's eyes and he smirked. "But I'll be back."

He leaned down and brushed a feather-light kiss across her lips, then straightened and headed out the door. His footsteps on the linoleum floor kept time with the EKG monitor until the sound disappeared completely, leaving her listening only to the erratic beat of her own heart.

"Well, that was way too touchy-feely for my taste," Cy said.

Josie relaxed her head back into the thin pillow, feeling about fifteen degrees warmer than she had a few minutes ago. "Shut up, Cy."

He opened his mouth to speak, but the woman at his side quieted him with another squeeze. He looked down at her and his expression shifted from annoyance to something much softer.

The other woman approached her bed, a kind smile dominating her heart-shaped face. "I'm so sorry to meet you under these circumstances. I'm Marlene Truss."

Everything clicked together. "The governor's daughter?" Cy had told her in Vegas he was protecting the governor's daughter from an assassination plot by the Callandriello family.

"Yes. If I'd have known everything that had happened was putting you in danger, I never would have let Cy come with me."

"Like you could have stopped me."

Marlene pushed her dark bangs from her face and stared up at Cy with her hands on her hips. She didn't say anything. She didn't have to. Cy, who stood at least a foot taller and was a hundred pounds heavier, grimaced and turned his attention back to his sister.

"Are you okay? How about the hand?"

"The doctors want me to stay another night, but after that, they said I'll be tired but recover completely. I'll be like my old self in a few days." She lifted her bandaged hand off the bed, staring at it as if it were an alien. "As to the hand, I have to wait and see, but I'll be painting again. The only way I'll give it up is if I lose all my fingers on both hands, and then I'll figure out how to paint with my toes."

"And is that what you plan to do? Go back to Vegas and paint?"

The plan gelled together in her head in an instant. It was perfect. She wanted him. He wanted her. Time to break out her kickass princess attitude and slay a dragon. "Hell no. I know exactly what I'm going to do." And it wasn't going to happen in Vegas.

# Chapter Twenty

The end of the lunch crowd filled The Harvest Bistro to capacity and Josie weaved her way between the tables with a nine-ounce steak and rosemary potato wedges drizzled with olive oil in one hand and pan-seared salmon with mixed greens in the other.

When the doctors told her she'd be right as rain within a month after leaving the hospital, she figured they were full of shit. But true to their word, she felt fine. Her right hand got tired easy, but Dr. Coll said that would go away in time too. It had been four weeks since she'd last seen Sam Layton in her hospital room.

Four very long weeks.

Not that she'd been sitting around waiting for his call or chasing after him. No. Her plan involved doing the one thing she was sure he never expected. Ignoring him. Eventually, he'd break, she was sure of it, but she didn't know how much longer she'd be able to hold out. Odds were she'd be knocking on his door in less than forty-eight hours.

In the meantime, she'd sweet-talked Celestine into renting out the studio cabin to her for the foreseeable future and had spent the majority of her time painting. The thought of going back to Vegas after all that had happened make her sick to her stomach. She liked the pace and friendliness of small town America. Of course, now she needed a job and she figured waiting tables in Dry Creek couldn't be that different than in Vegas. She'd been filling out an application to work at Harvest when the lunch crowd had swarmed the place, so she'd offered to help out until it slowed a bit.

"So has that son of mine shown his face yet?" Glenda Layton spread her napkin on her lap and glanced approvingly at her salmon.

"I haven't seen him." Josie put the steak in front of Bob Layton.

"No one has. I swear that boy has burrowed underground." She eyeballed her husband of forty years. "I thought you were going to have a talk with him."

"I did."

She tossed up her hands in frustration. "And?"

"We talked." He shrugged and concentrated on his lunch.

Glenda huffed. "Bob, getting information out of you is like pulling the teeth of a pissed-off bull."

"You always were full of piss and vinegar, Glenda. One of my favorite things about you." He started cutting his steak. "Well, that and your legs."

A shadow fell over the table.

Josie looked over her shoulder to see Sam wearing a bright-red sweater and jeans with worn cuffs. Bits of blue paint had dried in his hair.

God, he smelled delicious, like hot, sexy man. All she wanted to do was slide her hands underneath the cherry wool and touch his hard chest or, maybe, her hands would travel downward to the button on his jeans. She clenched her thighs together at the mental image.

He smirked at her as if he knew exactly what she was thinking and completely approved.

In a heartbeat, she decided to bolt before she lost her battle with self-control. "Okay then, I'm gonna run and see if the waitresses need any more help."

She spun on her heel to flee. Warm, strong fingers wrapped around hers. "How are you?"

*Nervous. Excited. Horny.* "I'm okay, how about you?"

"I meant, how are you feeling since you left the hospital?"

*Except for missing you? Perfect.* "I didn't believe the doctors when they said I'd be right as rain in a few weeks, but they were right. I couldn't take sitting around the cabin anymore and had to break out."

"I heard you're staying in Dry Creek."

"Yeah, despite everything, I like it here."

"I like it with you here too." He took a step closer, sexual energy coming off of him in waves. "And you already got a job, a place to live?"

Her clit throbbed between her legs. They'd never made it through a conversation without her wanting to drag him to the nearest horizontal location; hell, vertical would work too. "This is my audition, I guess you could say, so I better get back to it."

"I'll be waiting." He brought her hand up to his lips and kissed the tattoo on the inside of her wrist.

A shiver skipped down her spine and made everything south of the border tingle. "What if I don't want to talk with you? It *has* been a month."

"It's true I have a lot to make up for, but I think you'll give me an A-plus." His thumb caressed the spot where his lips had been.

God, she didn't realize just how much she'd missed his touch. Since the day they met, they hadn't been able to keep their hands to themselves. It was as if their bodies had known this was something special long before their own stubborn wills were willing to admit it. Her stomach flipped and flopped. This was the beginning and she couldn't wait to get started.

"Give me fifteen minutes."

Josie dropped off a few more orders, handed over her application to Claire and hunted down Sam in the dining room. She found him sitting at the bar in a side room, drinking a black cup of coffee.

Grinning like a fool in love, she sat down on the stool next to him. "Hey there, hot stuff."

He didn't answer, but instead slid a wooden rectangle across the mahogany bar to her. The length of a business envelope, the intricately carved box had an inlaid oak R in the middle of the lid. She caressed the letter and recognition hit her like a splash of water.

Rebecca's Bounty. The cave. With everything that had happened, she'd completely forgotten about it.

"How'd you get this?"

"Hank's deputies recovered it as evidence. With Snips' death, he closed the case and released everything. I told him I'd bring this to you."

"But it's not mine. This is your family's legacy." She glanced out at his parents, laughing about something as they ate their lunches. "Your mom, she'll want it."

"No. You found it. Whatever is in here, it's yours."

"You haven't opened it?"

"It's not mine to open."

Her hands shook as she fiddled with the latch. She pushed a lever and it clicked. The golden clasp popped open. Inside were several gold coins with the profile of a woman with flowing hair imprinted on them. She picked one up and held it in the palm of her hand. The word "liberty" and several stars were engraved on it, along with the year eighteen sixty-five.

Sam picked one of the coins up out of the box. "It's a Liberty Head gold coin. Rebecca must have brought them West with her from St. Louis."

A large bleached canvas pouch lay to one side. Its heft surprised her when she lifted it from its spot. She carefully untied the string at the top and reached inside, only to touch dozens of cool stones with sharp edges. When she pulled one out, the large bright-green emerald with small diamonds surrounding it shone in the light.

"Her earrings." She didn't even bother to try to keep the awe out of her voice.

"You should try them on." Sam pushed a curl behind her ear, exposing her lobe to his perusal. Lust and something that looked a lot like love brought out the gold in his tawny eyes and his thumb stroked her bare ear and trailed down her neck.

Although they'd seen much more of each other, the intimacy of the moment shook her.

"No way. I don't have the best record as of late. I can't imagine what would happen to these babies if wore them." She dropped the earring back in the pouch and handed it to Sam.

Only the velvet lining and a rolled-up piece of paper remained in Rebecca's treasure box. Slowly, she opened the scroll, revealing a charcoal sketch of McPherson's Bluff. With a few strokes Rebecca had managed to showcase the true depth and foreboding hope the bluff represented.

A chill sent goose bumps running up Josie's arms. "If it would be alright, I'd like to keep this."

"It's all yours. Everyone in the family agrees that the treasure belongs to you. People have spent decades looking for Rebecca's Bounty and you're the one who found it."

"But it's got to be worth—"

"A lot, yeah." He shrugged his broad shoulders.

Her mind raced. The gold and jewelry had to be worth millions. There had to be enough value in Rebecca's Bounty to finance several decades of painting, if not a lifetime. She'd be able to help with her mother's medical bills.

Finally, she was free to do whatever she wanted. Her whole life was about to change. She'd had to go through hell first, but everything had fallen into place. It wasn't just the treasure though, she'd found something much more valuable and completely unexpected. Sam.

"Look, you found it. It's yours. Take it as a sign that your luck is about to change." His stool screeched against the floor when he scooted back and stepped down. "Come on, there's something else I have to show you."

છ૰છ૰છ

"You wanted to show me your house?" Josie didn't know what she'd been expecting, but parking in front of Sam's one-story house sure wasn't it.

He laughed, the honeyed sound warming her from the inside out. His fingers held hers as they walked hand-in-hand to the front door. "Close your eyes."

The words tickled her ear and when she closed her eyes, all she could picture was her tongue flicking across his peach nipple. In response, her own nubs hardened against the smooth silk of her leopard-print bra.

"We're going to have to revisit this position." Sam pressed against her back, his rigid cock nestling in the crack of her ass. "I like making you guess what's going to happen next."

Sam reached past her and the click of the doorknob reached her sensitive ears. He eased her forward into the living room. Inside, he drew his lips down the side of her neck, ending with a gentle nip at her collarbone. "Take a look and tell me what you think."

Gone were the eggshell-white walls and bland window blinds. In their place were bright, pale lapis-blue walls and soft gray curtains. Her bottom lip shook and her heart went into overdrive. "This is the equivalent of some people going out and getting a full body tattoo."

"Yeah, I think I threw poor Ned at the hardware store into shock when I asked for a gallon of something besides white or cream."

"I can imagine that. But why did you do it?"

He took her face between his large palms, burying his fingers in her hair. "Because I've always been horrible at saying what I feel. In my defense, I've never had much to say about my emotions one way or another. With you, there's so much I want to say, but I just can't put it into words."

"You did just fine at the hospital."

He shook his head. "The exception that proves the rule." He paused, his gaze focusing on the painting of McPherson's Bluff above the couch as if he could find what he wanted to say hidden in the brush strokes. Expelling a deep breath, he turned his attention on her. "I'm not very good at saying how I feel about you, Josie, but I promise I'll always show you."

"I'll show you too." There were a million things Josie wanted to talk about, but it was the time for action. She leaned into him and captured his mouth, her tongue demanding entrance, and all the fear, uncertainty and hunger of the past few weeks rushed to the forefront.

Her hands snaked around him, sneaking underneath his soft red sweater. A T-shirt tucked into his jeans blocked her from skin-to-skin contact and she wanted to shred the cotton to get at him, to touch and taste his warm skin. She yanked the shirt from his jeans, exposing a slim patch of bare skin along his lower back. Electricity sparked between them, traveling from her fingertips to her clit in a bolt of passion. Weaving her hand between the cotton and his skin, she pushed the material higher, but not enough.

Sam broke the kiss and pushed her back a few inches, pulling his shirt and sweater off. "Take your clothes off."

The bass vibrations in his voice turned her belly into molten want. She smirked and trailed her fingers down the deep V of her emerald-green shirt. Enjoying the pained pleasure reflected in his hazel eyes, she inched her fingers over her right tit, lingering on her nipple, before heading south until she grasped the shirt's hem between two fingers.

"And what if I say no?"

His Adam's apple bobbed at her question, but he met her challenging stare with one of his own. "Then I'll rip it off you."

"That doesn't sound very professorial of you."

"Right now I'm not teaching you anything, I figure that game will come later—unless you want me to get out my ruler."

"Yes, sir." She whipped the shirt off and stood before him in her bra and low-slung jeans. Again, she caressed her sensitive skin on the way back down to the button on her jeans and watched his cock jump underneath his zipper. "I think you like watching me touch myself."

"God, yes."

She flicked the button open. "I've spent so many nights since Vegas imagining it was your fingers sliding into my wet slit, making me come. Then when you finally did touch me again, that night after we danced at Robidoux Roadhouse, you were even better than my fantasies."

Heat flushed his cheeks, deepening the pink of the new scar on his cheek, and he took a step forward. He grasped her waistband and yanked her to him.

Automatically, her hands went to his shoulders for balance. She skimmed her palms across his upper chest, his coarse hair rough against her delicate skin. Inhaling his musky scent, Josie tasted her way across his collarbone, ending with a nip on his pectoral muscle.

Sam's grip tightened on her jeans and he half moaned, half groaned her name. The sound only encouraged her to take it further and she scraped her nails across his shoulder blades, because making him lose some of that tightly guarded control turned her on. Rough and hard, he pulled her against his cock, rocking against her. Tension tightened in her belly as she met each stroke.

Fast as a whip, he turned her around and bent her over the back of the couch. Tall as she was, only the tips of her toes maintained contact with the floor.

"Are you sure you're up for this?" Sam pressed one hand between her shoulder blades, holding her in place with her ass in the air.

Anticipation rippled through her body. "As long as you're not planning to toss me into a walk-in freezer, we're all good."

"No, I'm going to keep you hot and wet for some time." He peeled her jeans off her legs, exposing the leopard-print thong framing her ass. Squeezing each globe, he pulled them apart. His thumb stroked down her wet center, her desire soaking her thong. "Fuck, Josie, you are so wet."

The thick digit pushed aside the silky material and sank into her pussy. Pleasure arched her back as tight as a bow and she pushed against his hand. She squeezed her eyes shut and concentrated on the little shivers making her body vibrate.

"Does that feel good?"

"Fuck yes."

He laughed and increased his speed. Bright colors appeared on the edges of her vision as the shivers grew in intensity.

The sound of a zipper lowering pierced through her euphoria. "You have my dick so hard right now. I'm going to slide it into your wet pussy, but not until you orgasm first. I want you to come all over my hand. Then I want you to taste the wetness on my fingers while you stroke my cock. That sound good to you?"

And the man said he didn't know how to put his feelings into words. Damn, if he kept this up he could make her climax from across the room with only his dirty talk and attitude.

His thumb slowed but the pressure increased and he added the additional sweet torment of two fingers sliding on either side of her hard clit. "You have to say something, Josie, or I'll have to stop. And I don't want to stop. I want to fuck you until my body has told you everything I can't. Do you understand me?"

She mewled her assent as every muscle tightened.

"Tell me you want that." He timed his thrusts with each word, going deeper and harder with each syllable. "Tell. Me."

"Yes." A lightning bolt of color snapped across her line of sight. Her walls clenched his thumb as her body became rigid with an orgasm that had her calling out his name.

Muscles melted, she slid down the couch, his arms around her, until they both ended up in a pile of naked limbs on the floor. The vibrant hues of her orgasm muted back into reality and her heart slowed to a normal rhythm as she rested her head on his bare chest.

Only Sam had ever made her come so hard the world glowed neon. That beat her solo fantasies by a long shot. Thinking of which, her nipples pointed at the memory of Sam's request, but he didn't make a move. Perhaps it was just the heat of the moment, or maybe he wasn't as confident in pushing boundaries as he'd said but she wasn't going to let it pass quietly into the night. They'd gone through too much together to go back to playing it soft and sweet.

Her hand snaked down to his and she raised it so that his thumb rested against the bottom lip of her open mouth. Watching his hazel eyes, she extended the tip of her tongue and licked the tangy wetness while circling her fingers around his hard cock. She closed her lips around his thumb and drew it into her mouth. His dick jumped in her hand. She squeezed and pumped it in a steady pace as she sucked his thumb clean.

Turning her focus to the prize in her hand, she spotted the pre-cum pooling on the tip. She leaned down and without slowing her pace, wiped the head across her lips as if she were putting on lipstick. Maintaining eye contact, she slowly and deliberately licked the liquid from her mouth.

She let go of his cock, reached around behind her and unhooked her bra, letting it drop to the floor. The hunger in his eyes started the electric buzz in her clit again. She stood up, spread her legs slightly more than shoulder-width apart and leaned over the back of the couch until her heavy breasts pressed against the back cushion. "Doesn't this pussy look good enough to fuck?"

Within two heartbeats, he was behind her burying his cock in her wetness. His strong hands clasped her hips, keeping her in place, as he slammed into her deep and at an angle that teased her G-spot. Her ass cheeks bounced with the impact of each stroke.

"You're so tight, so fucking good." He reached around and teasingly pinched her clit. "Come for me again. I want to feel you squeeze my cock with that hot pussy."

His fingers circled her nub in tight revolutions, robbing her of the ability to think or form words. All she could do was feel the pressure building inside her escalate to an almost painful level. Neon returned to the edges of her vision, brightening every hue to psychedelic levels.

She lifted her right leg, stretching it outward so her knee rested on the top of the couch. The change allowed him to plunge deeper inside her, every movement taking her closer and closer to release. The couch pressed painfully against her hipbones, but she was too close to try to adjust her position again. The colors heightened, blurring out everything else except for the kaleidoscope of glowing pigments as an orgasm shook her, body and soul.

"Oh my God, Josie." Sam's fingers bit into her flesh and he yanked her back one more time before his climax exploded and he collapsed on her.

It took a few minutes for the real world to invade with a trio of shivers that had nothing to do with sex, and a mountain of goose bumps across Josie's forearms.

Sam rubbed his hands across her arms. "Come on, let's get you under the covers so I can warm you up again."

Together they made their way into his bedroom, one wall now a burnt sienna. "My new favorite color."

"Oh yeah, why's that?"

Josie wrapped her arm around his waist, relishing the flex of muscle underneath her fingertips. "Because it makes me think of you."

# Epilogue

$\mathcal{J}$osie paused and stuck the end of the paintbrush in her mouth so she could stretch out the fingers on her right hand. She'd been at it for more than an hour, but something about the morning light in Sam's bedroom gave the rest of the world a soft glow, perfect for getting the image in her mind onto the canvas.

"Tell me again why I'm doing this," Sam grumbled from across the room.

He looked perfect, exactly as she'd imagined that first night in Vegas. "Because I've been wanting to paint you since the moment I saw you and you've turned over a new, more adventurous leaf."

"God, what was I thinking?"

Her concern he was really hating it evaporated the moment she looked up and saw the teasing glint in his hazel eyes. For the past month, he'd let his guard down a little bit more each day, and not just with her; his whole family had noticed the change. He'd even ordered something different for dinner at Juanita's, surprising the waiter so much that he'd spilled a drink.

She snarled her lip, mocking his sour expression. "Stop complaining and puff out your chest a little more."

Across the room, Sam stood in his bright-green boxers, one hand gripping a makeshift shield of a trashcan lid and the other holding a broom handle pointed out as if it were a spear. A ray of light landed on his head, turning his light-brown hair to the burnt sienna color that had first caught her eye in Vegas and matched the far wall. Perfect. She whipped the brush out of her mouth, dipped it in the paint on her palette and recreated the reddish hue in his hair.

Sam squinted his eyes and shifted his weight.

"You just had a break ten minutes ago, are you getting tired already?"

"Tired is not what I'm feeling." He adjusted his stance again.

"Oh come on, the eggs weren't that undercooked." But they had been a mess.

He shook his head. "Wrong again."

Her gaze dropped lower to the outline of his fast-hardening cock pressing against his boxers. An answering heat filled her and her nipples puckered under the thin cotton T-shirt. Then the light moved a smidgen, returning her attention to the Spartan warrior in front of her. "Damn, that looks good but I only have this light for a little bit longer."

"I'll give you fifteen minutes and then I'm going to extract revenge for making me stare at you dressed only in one of my old T-shirts for the past hour."

It was true, the threadbare white cotton undershirt barely reached her thighs and did nothing to disguise her freely swinging tits. Sam's revenge sounded very sweet.

"Now that sounds like fun."

"No, that sounds like your future." Flashing a grin that promised many wicked things, Sam winked at Josie.

"I can't wait."

# A Note From Avery

Hey you!

I really hope you enjoyed Sam and Josie! Nothing like finding love and millions of dollars worth of jewels. If you have a second to leave a review of Dangerous Tease, that would be awesome! Please stay in touch (avery@averyflynn.com), I love hearing from readers! Want to get all the latest book news? Subscribe to my newsletter for book gossip, monthly prizes and more! And don't forget to check out the other Layton books: Dangerous Kiss and Dangerous Flirt.

xoxo,

Avery

# Books By Avery Flynn

**The Killer Style Series**
*High-Heeled Wonder* (Killer Style 1)
*This Year's Black* (Killer Style 2)
*Make Me Up* (Killer Style 3)

**Sweet Salvation Brewery Series**
*Enemies on Tap* (Sweet Salvation Brewery 1)
*Hollywood on Tap* (Sweet Salvation Brewery 2)
*Trouble on Tap* (Sweet Salvation Brewery 3)

**Dangerous Love Series**
*Dangerous Kiss* (Laytons 1)
*Dangerous Flirt* (Laytons 2)
*Dangerous Tease* (Laytons 3)

**Novellas**
*Hot Dare*
*Betting the Billionaire*
*Jax and the Beanstalk Zombies* (Fairy True 1)
*Big Bad Red* (Fairy True 2)

## Newsletter

Subscribe to Avery's newsletter for news about her latest releases, giveaways and more!

## Street Team

Join the Flynnbots and get sneak peeks at Avery's latest books and more!

Visit Avery's website at www.averyflynn.com

Facebook: https://www.facebook.com/AveryFlynnAuthor

TSU: https://www.tsu.co/AveryFlynn

Pinterest: https://www.pinterest.com/averyflynnbooks/

Twitter: https://twitter.com/averyflynn

E-mail: avery@averyflynn.com